The Science Fiction Book Club COLLECTION

Ill Met in Lankhmar

FRITZ LEIBER

Illustrated by Bob Eggleton

Copyright © 1970 by The Estate of Fritz Leiber.
All rights reserved.

First published in *Fantasy and Science Fiction*.

Reprinted by arrangement with
White Wolf Publishing
780 Park North Boulevard
Suite 100
Clarkston, GA 30021

The characters and events described in this story are fictional. Any resemblance between a character herein and any person, living or dead, is purely coincidental.

Introduction copyright © 1996 by David G. Hartwell.

Jacket and interior art copyright © 1996 by Bob Eggleton.

ISBN: 1-56865-221-6

Printed in the United States of America

INTRODUCTION

"American Sword & Sorcery writers are in the Western European tradition," says Joanna Russ, "so they (and I) really reflect a kind of cultural ur-mind when they put together the Barbaric North (the homeland of Fafhrd, also Brak the Barbarian, Conan the Conqueror, Douglas the Dilittante, and all those other mighty-thewed persons) and the corrupt Southern urban culture to which the barbarian usually migrates. (Leiber's usual originality shows up well here—he uses one hero for each culture.)" Thus, she says, she likes to call the strange, archaic, barbaric-Hellenistic world of sword and sorcery Fritz Leiberland, after the writer whose works provide her favorite revelation of that setting, the tales of Fafhrd and the Gray Mouser.

"His own literary skills," says Michael Moorcock, "were generally far better than the majority of writers he admired . . . I once asked him why he wrote for commercial magazines whose audiences sometimes actively disliked his best work. He said that in the late '30s and '40s writers like himself—and he named Robert Bloch and Henry Kuttner amongst them—had no market at all, if they didn't have the pulp sf market. The literary market simply wasn't interested in their "surrealist" fantasies. So they adapted them to the pulp market and earned a little money while they learned."

Robert E. Howard created the most famous S&S hero, Conan, in the pulp magazine *Weird Tales* in the early 1930s, but in the end Fritz Leiber created the most influential works. Leiber was a cultured and literate writer, the son of a Shakespearean actor who went to Hollywood during the depression and made a living in the movies. His early works were signed Fritz Leiber, Jr., to distinguish him from his famous father. As a young man he was tall (6 foot 3 inches), blonde, handsome and articulate. He was married to Jonquil, a poet, who introduced him in correspondence to H.P. Lovecraft (to whom Leiber sent some of his early stories before publication). He made his living for much of the middle of his career as an editor for *Science Digest*.

Fame did not come quickly to Leiber, and the recognition of his fantasy writings arrived last. But they were the first fiction Leiber wrote and published.

In a 1962 essay introducing Fafhrd and the Gray Mouser, Leiber tells the engaging story of their creation in 1934: "Like true Depression children they didn't earn a cent for years and years—five years, to be exact.

"Jobs seemed impossible to come by and were often rather odd: during the past two years I had been hiring out as an Episcopalian minister; my friend

Harry Fischer had been putting on puppet shows featuring the chuckling murderer Punch and the grisly hangman Jack Ketch....

"In the summer of 1934 Harry Fischer had written to me from Louisville, Kentucky: 'I am static for fear that any motion would be fatal. The gods have laid my soul aside to moulder for a time,' and I had written to him from Atlantic Highlands, New Jersey: 'We still have those great foreknowledges of ourselves that you call adolescent fancies. But they will become mouldy and rotten and the trolls will creep into them greedily if we do not act soon.' "

Then in September Fischer wrote a letter to Leiber in which was embedded a description of two fictional characters: the Gray Mouser and Fafhrd. Leiber responded in kind. "We were using all our characters [Leiber mentions other characters the two had previously concocted] including Fafhrd and the Mouser, to comment on life and the affairs of the world," said Leiber.

"Fafhrd began as a somewhat regulation hero, though he has grown much less so. As for the Gray Mouser, one can point out faint similarities to Loki, Peer Gynt, François Villon, Etzel Andergast in Wassermann's Kerkhoven trilogy, Spendius in Flaubert's *Salammbo*, Jurgen himself and Horvendile in *The Cream of the Jest*, even the Pied Piper of Hamelin and Punch as a young man, but they are greatly outweighed by the differences—quite unconvincing. The Mouser stubbornly remains the Mouser alone.

"Authors, of course, inevitably put much of themselves into their characters. So in a sense Harry Fischer is the Gray Mouser and I am Fafhrd."

In two different essays on the 1930s and on the early stories, Leiber tells autobiographical anecdotes about meeting the great adventure film star, John Barrymore, whose real-life drinking and womanizing are legendary (and certainly impressed the young Leiber as much as Barrymore's articulate discourse on Poe and other literary figures). In addition to the insistent claim that Leiber is himself the basis of Fafhrd, one cannot resist the implication that some of Barrymore was projected into Fafhrd. It is certain, in any case, that Leiber began to behave more like Barrymore than like Fafhrd in the 1940s and 1950s.

Finally in 1939 Leiber sold "Two Sought Adventure", the first published story of the sequence and FL's first story, to *Unknown*, John W. Campbell, Jr.'s revolutionary fantasy magazine. The next major novella in the series, originally written in 1936 and rejected as "too full of stylistic novelties," had to wait until the 1947 collection, *Night's Black Agents*, to see print. The first collection of Fafhrd and the Gray Mouser tales appeared from a small press in 1957, *Two Sought Adventure*.

In the meantime Leiber became a well-known name in science fiction, especially for his novel, *Gather, Darkness* (serialized in *Astounding* in the early 1940s) and built a reputation as a revolutionary writer in the horror field for a number of contemporary urban supernatural stories published in *Unknown*. He was a crucial figure from the 1940s to the present in establishing contemporary and urban settings as a dominant feature of horror fiction. His early horror novel, *Conjure Wife*, is considered a classic. "It became a familiar refrain, amongst Leiber enthusiasts," says Moorcock, "that he was too good for his markets, and that he was ahead of his time. Both these things were to some extent true: The markets of those days were far less sophisticated than those of today and a lot of sf readers—who made up the majority in an extremely small market—were deeply conservative, actively disliking anything which was not the "hard" sf of the kind appearing in *Astounding* (later *Analog*) and believing Sword & Sorcery to be an illogical and unwholesome abomination. Amongst the horror fans, any form of humour was regarded almost as blasphemy."

Then at the start of the 1950s he had a revolutionary impact on the science fiction field with his stories, "Coming Attraction" and "Poor Superman." The first of these could easily be seen as one of the wellsprings of cyberpunk sf, decades later in the 1980s, the second as a parody of John W. Campbell, Jr. and L. Ron Hubbard, and both are more or less direct attacks on the established attitudes of Golden Age Campbellian science fiction, the attitudes that dominated the 1940s. Critics such as Algis Budrys credit Leiber with breaking down the walls and freeing up the writers of the 1950s. Leiber wrote the stories, did it well, got them published and the barriers evaporated—many others followed, in the new magazines of the 1950s such as *Galaxy* and *The Magazine of Fantasy and Science Fiction*.

Leiber did not return to writing Fafhrd and the Gray Mouser pieces until the early 1960s. This was the time in which the Sword & Sorcery adventures of Robert E. Howard's Conan the Barbarian from the 1930s were reprinted, ordered, and expanded by others in paperback, achieving enormous popularity. Cele Goldsmith, the innovative editor of *Fantastic* and the first woman ever to win the Hugo Award as best editor, encouraged Leiber to continue the fantasy series and he responded with enthusiasm. New Fafhrd and Gray Mouser stories began to appear. Then in 1968 Leiber ordered the stories and began to collect them under the auspices of editor Donald A. Wollheim at Ace Books.

Ultimately the series includes seven volumes: *Swords and Deviltry* (collected 1970), *Two Sought Adventure* (collected 1957; expanded and revised as *Swords Against Death* 1970), *Swords in the Mist* (collected 1968), *Swords Against*

Wizardry (collected 1968), *The Swords of Lankhmar* (1961 *Fantastic* as "Scylla's Daughter"; expanded as a novel, 1968), *Swords and Ice Magic* (collected 1970), *The Knight and Knave of Swords* (collected 1988).

The Encyclopedia of Science Fiction says of the series:

"The series developed into a complex and enjoyable cycle owing little to the standard cliches of its subgenre (Leiber is credited with coining the widely used descriptive name, Sword & Sorcery). The mood varies from sombre introspection to broad comedy, and there is a very wide range of invention. On its original publication, the long story "Ill Met in Lankhmar" (1970 in *Swords and Deviltry*) won both Hugo and Nebula awards. *The Swords of Lankhmar*, which adds a strong element of sophisticated fetishistic sex to its other virtues—as does the book-length title story in *The Knight and Knave of Swords*—has strong claims to be considered the best modern heroic-fantasy novel, as well as Leiber's own best novel."

"Ill Met in Lankhmar" remains one of Leiber's best stories. It is one of his later pieces, written more than thirty years after the earliest ones, but still nearly twenty years before the last. It was written to fill in a specific gap in the ordering of the whole overarching series—it is the story of how the two companions first meet and become a duo. There is then no finer introduction to the fantasy world and its inhabitants than this tale. It is a rich treat, on a par with having your first Chinese food or attending your first live concert. Think of how many more occasions you might have to return to this venue (this is the appeal of a series).

Of the twentieth century's Grand Masters, Fritz Leiber is the only one to have been awarded that title in the three genres that have been associated in the SF field: science fiction, fantasy and horror. He won the Hugo Award, the Nebula Award, and the World Fantasy Award each several times, and an uncounted number of other awards during his distinguished and influential career. He became known first as a science fiction and horror writer, but in the end was most popular and famous as the author of the tales of Fafhrd and the Gray Mouser. These stories (and one novel) are generally regarded as the best series ever written in the subgenre of heroic fantasy known as Sword & Sorcery.

—David G. Hartwell
Pleasantville, N.Y.

ILL MET IN LANKHMAR

Silent as specters, the tall and the fat thief edged past the dead, noose-strangled watch-leopard, out the thick, lock-picked door of Jengao the Gem Merchant, and strolled east on Cash Street through the thin black night-smog of Lankhmar, City of Sevenscore Thousand Smokes.

East on Cash it had to be, for west at the intersection of Cash and Silver was a police post with unbribed guardsmen in browned-iron cuirasses and helms, restlessly grounding and rattling their pikes, while Jengao's place had no alley entrance or even window in its stone walls three spans thick and the roof and floor almost as strong and without trap doors.

But tall, tight-lipped Slevyas, master thief candidate, and fat, darting-eyed Fissif, thief second class, brevetted first class for this operation, with a rating of talented in double-dealing, were not in the least worried. Everything was proceeding according to plan. Each carried thonged in his pouch a much smaller pouch of jewels of the first water only, for Jengao, now breathing stentoriously inside and senseless from the slugging he'd suffered, must be allowed, nay, nursed and encouraged, to build up his business again and so ripen it for another plucking. Almost the first law of the Thieves' Guild was never kill the hen that laid brown eggs with a ruby in the yolk, or white eggs with a diamond in the white.

The two thieves also had the relief of knowing that, with the satisfaction of a job well done, they were going straight home now, not to a wife, Aarth forbid!—or to parents and children, all gods forfend!—but to Thieves' House, headquarters and barracks of the all-mighty Guild which was father to them both and mother too, though no woman was allowed inside its ever-open portal on Cheap Street.

In addition there was the comforting

knowledge that although each was armed only with his regulation silver-hilted thief's knife, a weapon seldom used except in rare intramural duels and brawls, in fact more a membership token than a weapon, they were nevertheless most strongly convoyed by three reliable and lethal bravos hired for the evening from the Slayers' Brotherhood, one moving well ahead of them as point, the other two well behind as rear guard and chief striking force, in fact almost out of sight—for it is never wise that such convoying be obvious, or so believed Krovas, Grandmaster of the Thieves' Guild.

And if all that were not enough to make Slevyas and Fissif feel safe and serene, there danced along soundlessly beside them in the shadow of the north curb a small, malformed or at any rate somewhat large-headed shape that might have been a small dog, a somewhat undersized cat, or a very big rat. Occasionally it scuttled familiarly and even encouragingly a

little way toward their snugly felt-slippered feet, though it always scurried swiftly back into the darker dark.

True, this last guard was not an absolutely unalloyed reassurance. At that very moment, scarcely twoscore paces yet from Jengao's, Fissif tautly walked for a bit on tiptoe and strained his pudgy lips upward to whisper softly in Slevyas' long-lobed ear, "Damned if I like being dogged by that familiar of Hristomilo, no matter what security he's supposed to afford us. Bad enough that Krovas employs or lets himself be cowed into employing a sorcerer of most dubious, if dire, reputation and aspect, but that—"

"Shut your trap!" Slevyas hissed still more softly.

Fissif obeyed with a shrug and occupied himself even more restlessly and keenly than was his wont in darting his gaze this way and that, but chiefly ahead.

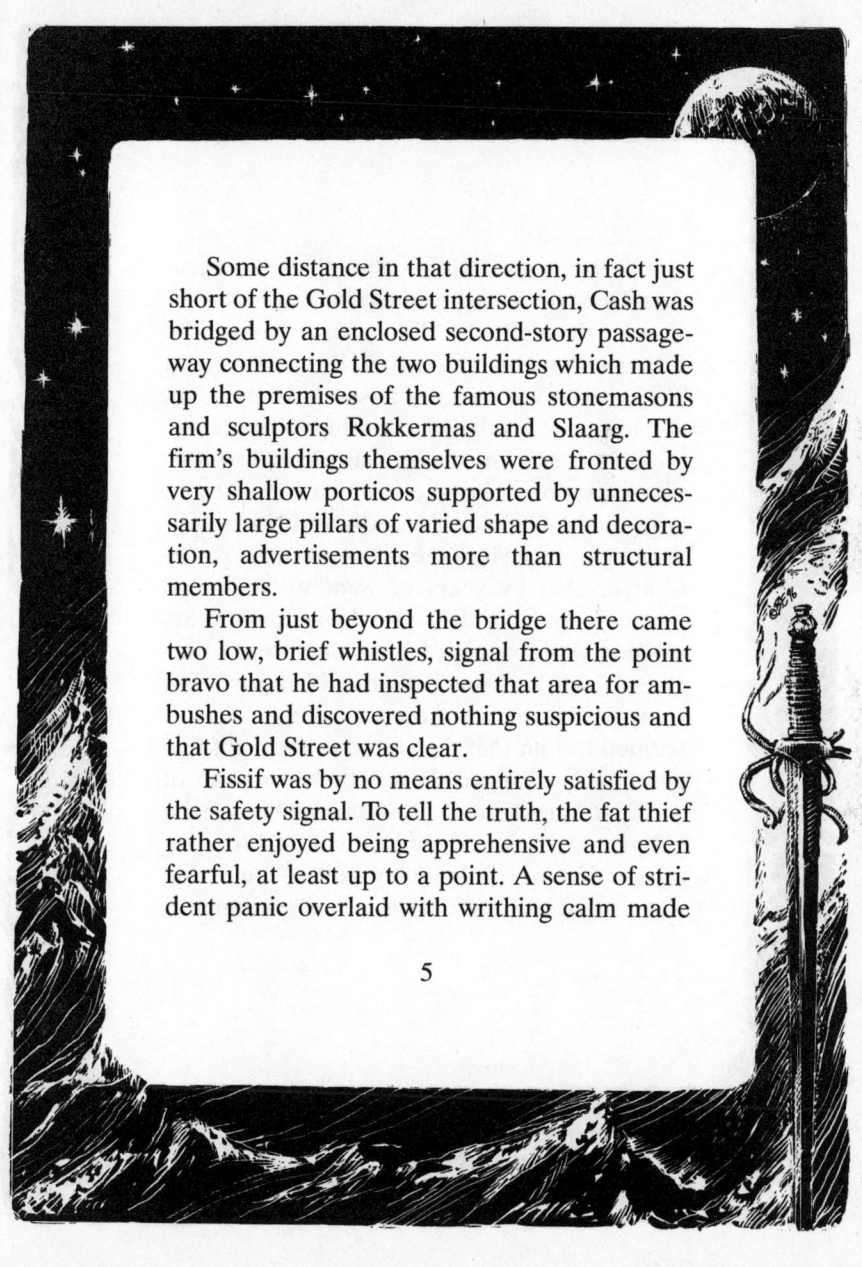

Some distance in that direction, in fact just short of the Gold Street intersection, Cash was bridged by an enclosed second-story passageway connecting the two buildings which made up the premises of the famous stonemasons and sculptors Rokkermas and Slaarg. The firm's buildings themselves were fronted by very shallow porticos supported by unnecessarily large pillars of varied shape and decoration, advertisements more than structural members.

From just beyond the bridge there came two low, brief whistles, signal from the point bravo that he had inspected that area for ambushes and discovered nothing suspicious and that Gold Street was clear.

Fissif was by no means entirely satisfied by the safety signal. To tell the truth, the fat thief rather enjoyed being apprehensive and even fearful, at least up to a point. A sense of strident panic overlaid with writhing calm made him feel more excitingly alive than the occasional woman he enjoyed. So he scanned most closely through the thin, sooty smog the frontages and overhangs of Rokkermas and Slaarg as his and Slevyas' leisurely seeming yet un-slow pace brought them steadily closer.

On this side the bridge was pierced by four small windows, between which were three large niches in which stood—another advertisement—three life-size plaster statues, somewhat eroded by years of weather and dyed varyingly tones of dark gray by as many years of smog. Approaching Jengao's before the burglary, Fissif had noted them with a swift but comprehensive overshoulder glance. Now it seemed to him that the statue to the right had indefinably changed. It was that of a man of medium height wearing cloak and hood, who gazed down with crossed arms and brooding aspect. No, not indefinably quite—the statue was a more uniform dark gray now, he fancied,

cloak, hood, and face; it seemed somewhat sharper featured, less eroded; and he would almost swear it had grown shorter!

Just below the niche, moreover, there was a scattering of gray and raw white rubble which he didn't recall having been there earlier. He strained to remember if during the excitement of the burglary, with its lively leopard-slaying and slugging and all, the unsleeping watch-corner of his mind had recorded a distant crash, and now he believed it had. His quick imagination pictured the possibility of a hole or even door behind each statue, through which it might be given a strong push and so tumbled onto passersby, himself and Slevyas specifically, the right-hand statue having been crashed to test the device and then replaced with a near twin.

He would keep close watch on all three statues as he and Slevyas walked under. It would be easy to dodge if he saw one start to

overbalance. Should he yank Slevyas out of harm's way when that happened? It was something to think about.

Without pause his restless attention fixed next on the porticos and pillars. The latter, thick and almost three yards tall, were placed at irregular intervals as well as being irregularly shaped and fluted, for Rokkermas and Slaarg were most modern and emphasized the unfinished look, randomness, and the unexpected.

Nevertheless it seemed to Fissif, his wariness wide awake now, that there was an intensification of unexpectedness, specifically that there was one more pillar under the porticos than when he had last passed by. He couldn't be sure which pillar was the newcomer, but he was almost certain there was one.

Share his suspicions with Slevyas? Yes, and get another hissed reproof and flash of contempt from the small, dull-seeming eyes.

The enclosed bridge was close now. Fissif glanced up at the right-hand statue and noted other differences from the one he'd recalled. Although shorter, it seemed to hold itself more strainingly erect, while the frown carved in its dark gray face was not so much one of philosophic brooding as sneering contempt, self-conscious cleverness, and conceit.

Still, none of the three statues toppled forward as he and Slevyas walked under the bridge. However, something else happened to Fissif at that moment. One of the pillars winked at him.

The Gray Mouser—for so Mouse now named himself to himself and Ivrian—turned around in the right-hand niche, leaped up and caught hold of the cornice, silently vaulted to the flat roof, and crossed it precisely in time to see the two thieves emerge below.

Without hesitation he leaped forward and down, his body straight as a crossbow bolt, the

soles of his ratskin boots aimed at the shorter thief's fat buried shoulder blades, though leading him a little to allow for the yard he'd walk while the Mouser hurtled toward him.

In the instant that he leaped, the tall thief glanced up overshoulder and whipped out a knife, though making no move to push or pull Fissif out of the way of the human projectile speeding toward him. The Mouser shrugged in full flight. He'd just have to deal with the tall thief faster after knocking down the fat one.

More swiftly than one would have thought he could manage, Fissif whirled around then and thinly screamed, "Slivikin!"

The ratskin boots took him high in the belly. It was like landing on a big cushion. Writhing aside from Slevyas' first thrust, the Mouser somersaulted forward, turning feet over head, and as the fat thief's skull hit a cobble with a dull bong he came to his feet with

dirk in hand, ready to take on the tall one. But there was no need. Slevyas, his small eyes glazed, was toppling too.

One of the pillars had sprung forward, trailing a voluminous robe. A big hood had fallen back from a youthful face and long-haired head. Brawny arms had emerged from the long, loose sleeves that had been the pillar's topmost section, while the big fist ending one of the arms had dealt Slevyas a shrewd knockout punch on the chin.

Fafhrd and the Gray Mouser faced each other across the two thieves sprawled senseless. They were poised for attack, yet for the moment neither moved.

Each discerned something inexplicably familiar in the other.

Fafhrd said, "Our motives for being here seem identical."

"Seem? Surely must be!" the Mouser answered curtly, fiercely eyeing this potential new foe, who was taller by a head than the tall thief.

"You said?"

"I said, 'Seem? Surely must be!'"

"How civilized of you!" Fafhrd commented in pleased tones.

"Civilized?" the Mouser demanded suspiciously, gripping his dirk tighter.

"To care, in the eye of action, exactly what's said," Fafhrd explained. Without letting the Mouser out of his vision, he glanced down. His gaze traveled from the belt and pouch of one fallen thief to those of the other. Then he looked up at the Mouser with a broad, ingenuous smile.

"Sixty-sixty?" he suggested.

The Mouser hesitated, sheathed his dirk, and rapped out, "A deal!" He knelt abruptly, his fingers on the drawstrings of Fissif's pouch. "Loot you Slivikin," he directed.

It was natural to suppose that the fat thief

had been crying his companion's name at the end. Without looking up from where he knelt, Fafhrd remarked, "That . . . ferret they had with them. Where did it go?"

"Ferret?" the Mouser answered briefly. "It was a marmoset!"

"Marmoset," Fafhrd mused. "That's a small tropical monkey, isn't it? Well, might have been, but I got the strange impression that—"

The silent, two-pronged rush which almost overwhelmed them at that instant really surprised neither of them. Each had been expecting it, but the expectation had dropped out of conscious thought with the startlement of their encounter.

The three bravos racing down upon them in concerted attack, two from the west and one from the east, all with swords poised to thrust, had assumed that the two highjackers would be armed at most with knives and as timid or at least cautious in weapons-combat as the gen-

eral run of thieves and counter-thieves. So it was they who were surprised and thrown into confusion when with the lightning speed of youth the Mouser and Fafhrd sprang up, whipped out fearsomely long swords, and faced them back to back.

The Mouser made a very small parry in carte so that the thrust of the bravo from the east went past his left side by only a hair's breath. He instantly riposted. His adversary, desperately springing back, parried in turn in carte. Hardly slowing, the tip of the Mouser's long, slim sword dropped under that parry with the delicacy of a princess curtsying and then leaped forward and a little upward, the Mouser making an impossibly long-looking lunge for one so small, and went between two scales of the bravo's armored jerkin and between his ribs and through his heart and out his back as if all were angelfood cake.

Meanwhile Fafhrd, facing the two bravos

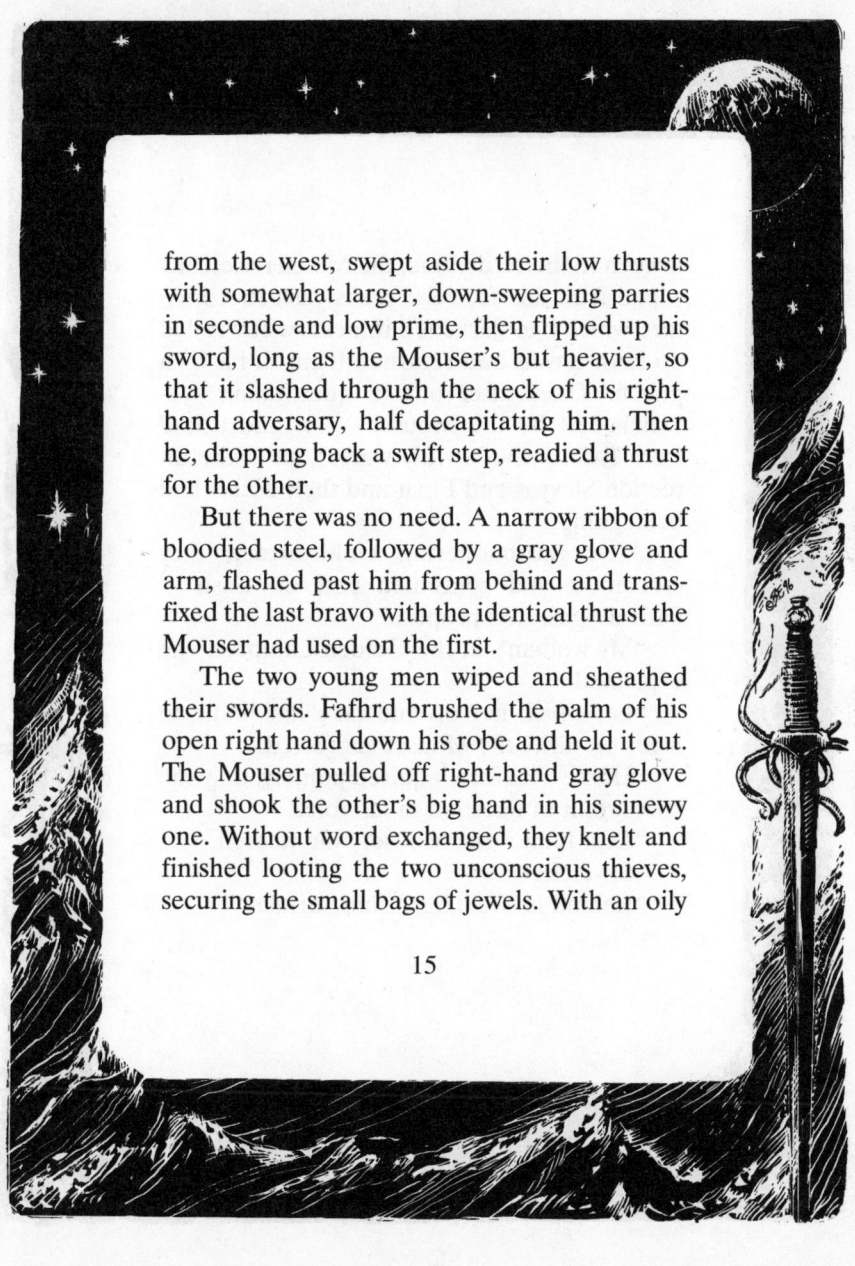

from the west, swept aside their low thrusts with somewhat larger, down-sweeping parries in seconde and low prime, then flipped up his sword, long as the Mouser's but heavier, so that it slashed through the neck of his right-hand adversary, half decapitating him. Then he, dropping back a swift step, readied a thrust for the other.

But there was no need. A narrow ribbon of bloodied steel, followed by a gray glove and arm, flashed past him from behind and transfixed the last bravo with the identical thrust the Mouser had used on the first.

The two young men wiped and sheathed their swords. Fafhrd brushed the palm of his open right hand down his robe and held it out. The Mouser pulled off right-hand gray glove and shook the other's big hand in his sinewy one. Without word exchanged, they knelt and finished looting the two unconscious thieves, securing the small bags of jewels. With an oily towel and then a dry one, the Mouser sketchily wiped from his face the greasy ash-soot mixture which had darkened it, next swiftly rolled up both towels and returned them to his own pouch. Then, after only a questioning eye-twitch east on the Mouser's part and a nod from Fafhrd, they swiftly walked on in the direction Slevyas and Fissif and their escort had been going.

After reconnoitering Gold Street, they crossed it and continued east on Cash at Fafhrd's gestured proposal.

"My woman's at the Golden Lamprey," he explained.

"Let's pick her up and take her home to meet my girl," the Mouser suggested.

"Home?" Fafhrd inquired politely, only the barest hint of question in his voice.

"Dim Lane," the Mouser volunteered.

"Silver Eel?"

"Behind it. We'll have some drinks."

"I'll pick up a jug. Never have too much juice."

"True. I'll let you."

Several squares farther on Fafhrd, after stealing a number of looks at his new comrade, said with conviction, "We've met before."

The Mouser grinned at him. "Beach by the Mountains of Hunger?"

"Right! When I was a pirate's ship-boy."

"And I was a wizard's apprentice."

Fafhrd stopped, again wiped right hand on robe, and held it out. "Name's Fafhrd. Ef ay ef aitch ar dee."

Again the Mouser shook it. "Gray Mouser," he said a touch defiantly, as if challenging anyone to laugh at the sobriquet. "Excuse me, but how exactly do you pronounce that? Faf-hrud?"

"Just Faf-erd."

"Thank you." They walked on.

"Gray Mouser, eh?" Fafhrd remarked.

"Well, you killed yourself a couple of rats tonight."

"That I did." The Mouser's chest swelled and he threw back his head. Then with a comic twitch of his nose and a sidewise half-grin he admitted, "You'd have got your second man easily enough. I stole him from you to demonstrate my speed. Besides, I was excited."

Fafhrd chuckled. "You're telling me? How do you suppose I was feeling?"

Later, as they were crossing Pimp Street, he asked, "Learn much magic from your wizard?"

Once more the Mouser threw back his head. He flared his nostrils and drew down the corners of his lips, preparing his mouth for boastful, mystifying speech. But once more he found himself twitching his nose and half grinning. What the deuce did this big fellow have that kept him from putting on his usual acts? "Enough to tell me it's damned dangerous stuff. Though I still fool with it now and then."

Fafhrd was asking himself a similar question. All his life he'd mistrusted small men, knowing his height awakened their instant jealousy. But this clever little chap was somehow an exception. Quick thinker and brilliant swordsman too, no argument. He prayed to Kos that Vlana would like him.

On the northeast corner of Cash and Whore a slow-burning torch shaded by a broad gilded hoop cast a cone of light up into the thickening black night-smog and another cone down on the cobbles before the tavern door. Out of the shadows into the second cone stepped Vlana, handsome in a narrow black velvet dress and red stockings, her only ornaments a silver-sheathed and hilted dagger and a silver-worked black pouch, both on a plain black belt.

Fafhrd introduced the Gray Mouser, who behaved with an almost fawning courtesy, obsequiously gallant. Vlana studied him boldly,

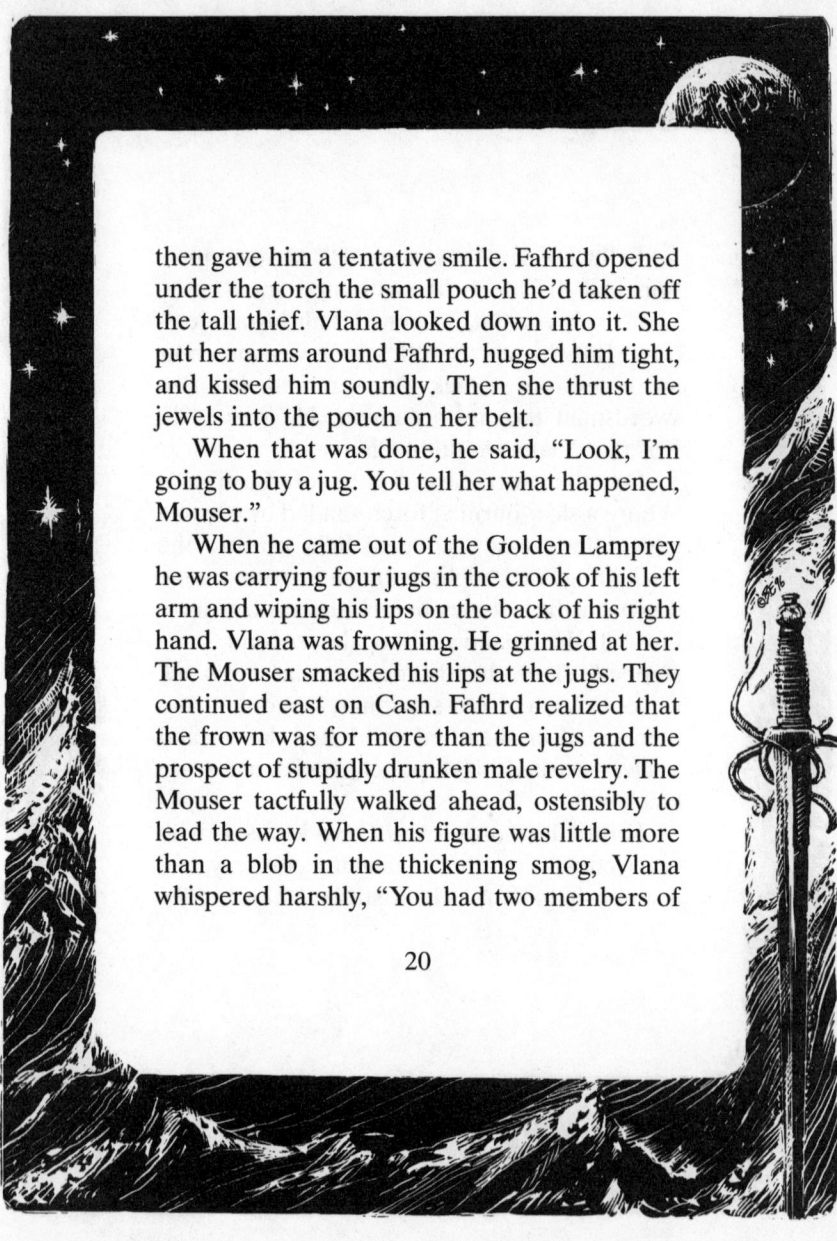

then gave him a tentative smile. Fafhrd opened under the torch the small pouch he'd taken off the tall thief. Vlana looked down into it. She put her arms around Fafhrd, hugged him tight, and kissed him soundly. Then she thrust the jewels into the pouch on her belt.

When that was done, he said, "Look, I'm going to buy a jug. You tell her what happened, Mouser."

When he came out of the Golden Lamprey he was carrying four jugs in the crook of his left arm and wiping his lips on the back of his right hand. Vlana was frowning. He grinned at her. The Mouser smacked his lips at the jugs. They continued east on Cash. Fafhrd realized that the frown was for more than the jugs and the prospect of stupidly drunken male revelry. The Mouser tactfully walked ahead, ostensibly to lead the way. When his figure was little more than a blob in the thickening smog, Vlana whispered harshly, "You had two members of

the Thieves' Guild knocked out cold and you didn't cut their throats?"

"We slew three bravos," Fafhrd protested by way of excuse.

"My quarrel is not with the Slayers' Brotherhood, but that abominable Guild. You swore to me that whenever you had the chance—"

"Vlana! I couldn't have the Gray Mouser thinking I was an amateur counter-thief consumed by hysteria and blood lust."

"You already set great store by him, don't you?"

"He possibly saved my life tonight."

"Well, he told me that *he'd* have slit their throats in a wink, if he'd known I wanted it that way."

"He was only playing up to you from courtesy."

"Perhaps and perhaps not. But *you* knew and you didn't—"

"Vlana, shut up!"

Her frown became a rageful glare, then suddenly she laughed wildly, smiled twitchingly as if she were about to cry, mastered herself and smiled more lovingly. "Pardon me, darling," she said. "Sometimes you must think I'm going mad and sometimes I believe I am."

"Well, don't," he told her shortly. "Think of the jewels we've won instead. And behave yourself with our new friends. Get some wine inside you and relax. I mean to enjoy myself tonight. I've earned it."

She nodded and clutched his arm in agreement and for comfort and sanity. They hurried to catch up with the dim figure ahead.

The Mouser, turning left, led them a half square north on Cheap Street to where a narrower way went east again. The black mist in it looked solid.

"Dim Lane," the Mouser explained.

Fafhrd nodded that he knew.

Vlana said, "Dim's too weak—too *transparent* a word for it tonight," with an uneven laugh in which there were still traces of hysteria and which ended in a fit of strangled coughing. When she could swallow again, she gasped out, "Damn Lankhmar's night-smog! What a hell of a city."

"It's the nearness here of the Great Salt Marsh," Fafhrd explained. And he did indeed have part of the answer. Lying low betwixt the Marsh, the Inner Sea, the River Hlal, and the flat southern grain fields watered by canals fed by the Hlal, Lankhmar with its innumerable smokes was the prey of fogs and sooty smogs. No wonder the citizens had adopted the black toga as their formal garb. Some averred the toga had originally been white or pale brown, but so swiftly soot-blackened, necessitating endless laundering, that a thrifty Overlord had ratified and made official what nature or civilization's arts decreed.

About halfway to Carter Street, a tavern on the north side of the lane emerged from the murk. A gape-jawed serpentine shape of pale metal crested with soot hung high for a sign. Beneath it they passed a door curtained with begrimed leather, the slit in which spilled out noise, pulsing torchlight, and the reek of liquor.

Just beyond the Silver Eel the Mouser led them through an inky passageway outside the tavern's east wall. They had to go single file, feeling their way along rough, slimily bemisted brick and keeping close together.

"Mind the puddle," the Mouser warned. "It's deep as the Outer Sea."

The passageway widened. Reflected torchlight filtering down through the dark mist allowed them to make out only the most general shape of their surroundings. To the right was more windowless, high wall. To the left, crowding close to the back of the Silver Eel, rose a dismal, rickety building of darkened brick and blackened, ancient wood. It looked utterly deserted to Fafhrd and Vlana until they had craned back their heads to gaze at the fourth-story attic under the ragged-guttered roof. There faint lines and points of yellow light shone around and through three tightly-latticed windows. Beyond, crossing the T of the space they were in, was a narrow alley.

"Bones Alley," the Mouser told them in somewhat lofty tones. "I call it Ordure Boulevard."

"I can smell that," Vlana said.

By now she and Fafhrd could see a long, narrow wooden outside stairway, steep yet sagging and without a rail, leading up to the lighted attic. The Mouser relieved Fafhrd of the jugs and went up it quite swiftly.

"Follow me when I've reached the top," he called back. "I think it'll take your weight, Fafhrd, but best one of you at a time."

Fafhrd gently pushed Vlana ahead. With another hysteria-tinged laugh and a pause midway up for another fit of choked coughing, she mounted to the Mouser where he now stood in an open doorway, from which streamed yellow light that died swiftly in the night-smog. He was lightly resting a hand on a big, empty, wrought-iron lamp-hook firmly set in a stone section of the outside wall. He bowed aside, and she went in.

Fafhrd followed, placing his feet as close as he could to the wall, his hands ready to grab for support. The whole stairs creaked ominously and each step gave a little as he shifted his weight onto it. Near the top, one gave way with the muted crack of half-rotted wood. Gently as he could, he sprawled himself hand and knee on as many steps as he could reach, to distribute his weight, and cursed sulfurously.

"Don't fret, the jugs are safe," the Mouser called down gayly.

Fafhrd crawled the rest of the way, a somewhat sour look on his face, and did not get to his feet until he was inside the doorway. When he had done so, he almost gasped with surprise. It was like rubbing the verdigris from a cheap brass ring and finding a rainbow-fired diamond of the first water set in it. Rich drapes, some twinkling with embroidery of silver and gold, covered the walls except where the shuttered windows were—and the shutters of those were gilded. Similar but darker fabrics hid the low ceiling, making a gorgeous canopy in which the flecks of gold and silver were like stars. Scattered about were plump cushions and low tables, on which burned a multitude of candles. On shelves against the walls were neatly stacked like small logs a vast reserve of candles, numerous scrolls, jugs, bottles, and enameled boxes. A low vanity table was backed by a mirror of honed silver and thickly scattered over with jewels and cosmet-

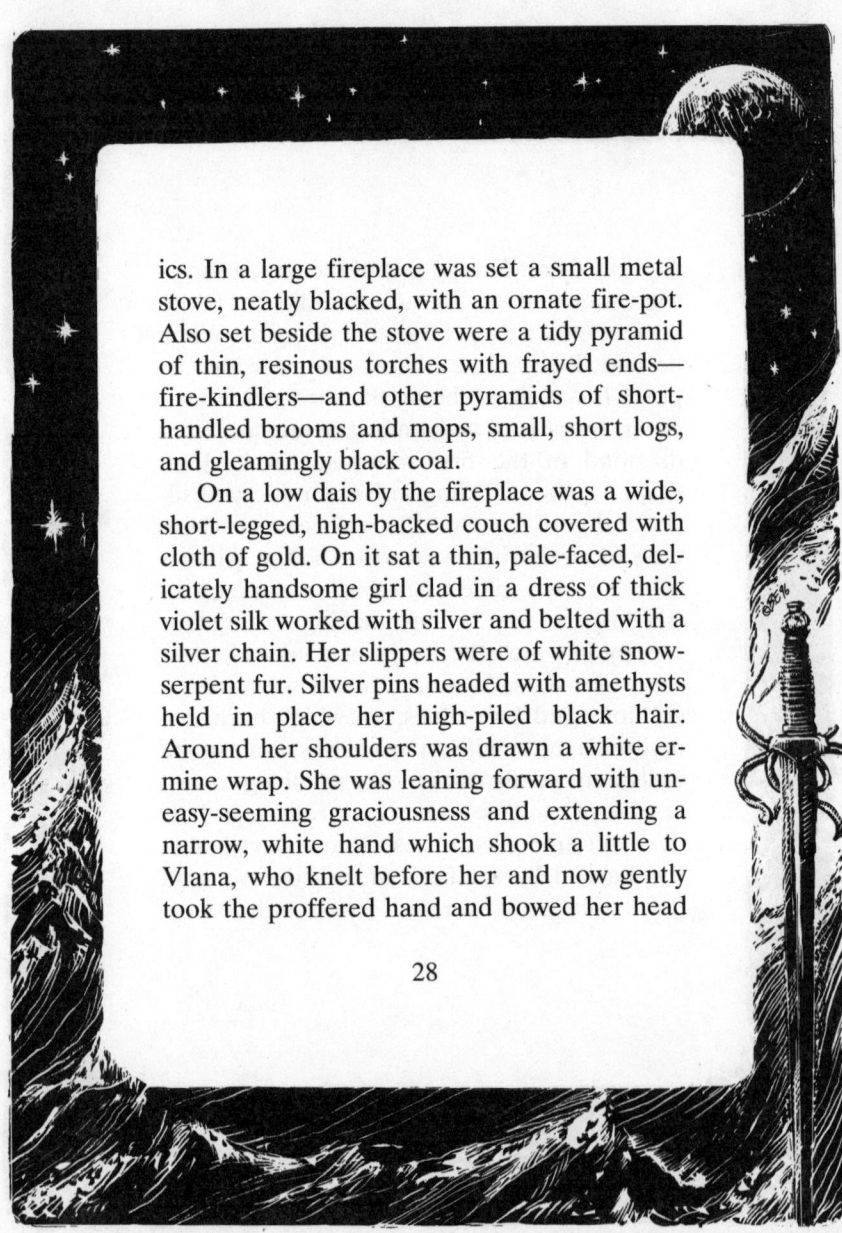

ics. In a large fireplace was set a small metal stove, neatly blacked, with an ornate fire-pot. Also set beside the stove were a tidy pyramid of thin, resinous torches with frayed ends— fire-kindlers—and other pyramids of short-handled brooms and mops, small, short logs, and gleamingly black coal.

On a low dais by the fireplace was a wide, short-legged, high-backed couch covered with cloth of gold. On it sat a thin, pale-faced, delicately handsome girl clad in a dress of thick violet silk worked with silver and belted with a silver chain. Her slippers were of white snow-serpent fur. Silver pins headed with amethysts held in place her high-piled black hair. Around her shoulders was drawn a white ermine wrap. She was leaning forward with uneasy-seeming graciousness and extending a narrow, white hand which shook a little to Vlana, who knelt before her and now gently took the proffered hand and bowed her head over it, her own glossy, straight, dark-brown hair making a canopy, and pressed the other girl's hands back to her lips.

Fafhrd was happy to see his woman playing up properly to this definitely odd though delightful situation. Then looking at Vlana's long, red-stockinged leg stretched far behind her as she knelt on the other, he noted that the floor was everywhere strewn—to the point of double, treble, and quadruple overlaps—with thick-piled, close-woven, many-hued rugs of the finest imported from the Eastern Lands. Before he knew it, his thumb had shot toward the Gray Mouser.

"You're the Rug Robber!" he proclaimed. "You're the Carpet Crimp!—and the Candle Corsair too," he continued, referring to two series of unsolved thefts which had been on the lips of all Lankhmar when he and Vlana had arrived a moon ago.

The Mouser shrugged impassive-faced at

Fafhrd, then suddenly grinned, his slitted eyes a-twinkle, and broke into an impromptu dance which carried him whirling and jigging around the room and left him behind Fafhrd, where he deftly reached down the hooded and long-sleeved huge robe from the latter's stooping shoulders, shook it out, carefully folded it, and set it on a pillow.

After a long, uncertain pause, the girl in violet nervously patted with her free hand the cloth of gold beside her and Vlana seated herself there, carefully not too close, and the two women spoke together in low voices, Vlana taking the lead, though not obviously.

The Mouser took off his own gray, hooded cloak, folded it almost fussily, and laid it beside Fafhrd's. Then they unbelted their swords, and the Mouser set them atop folded robe and cloak.

Without those weapons and bulking garments, the two men looked suddenly like

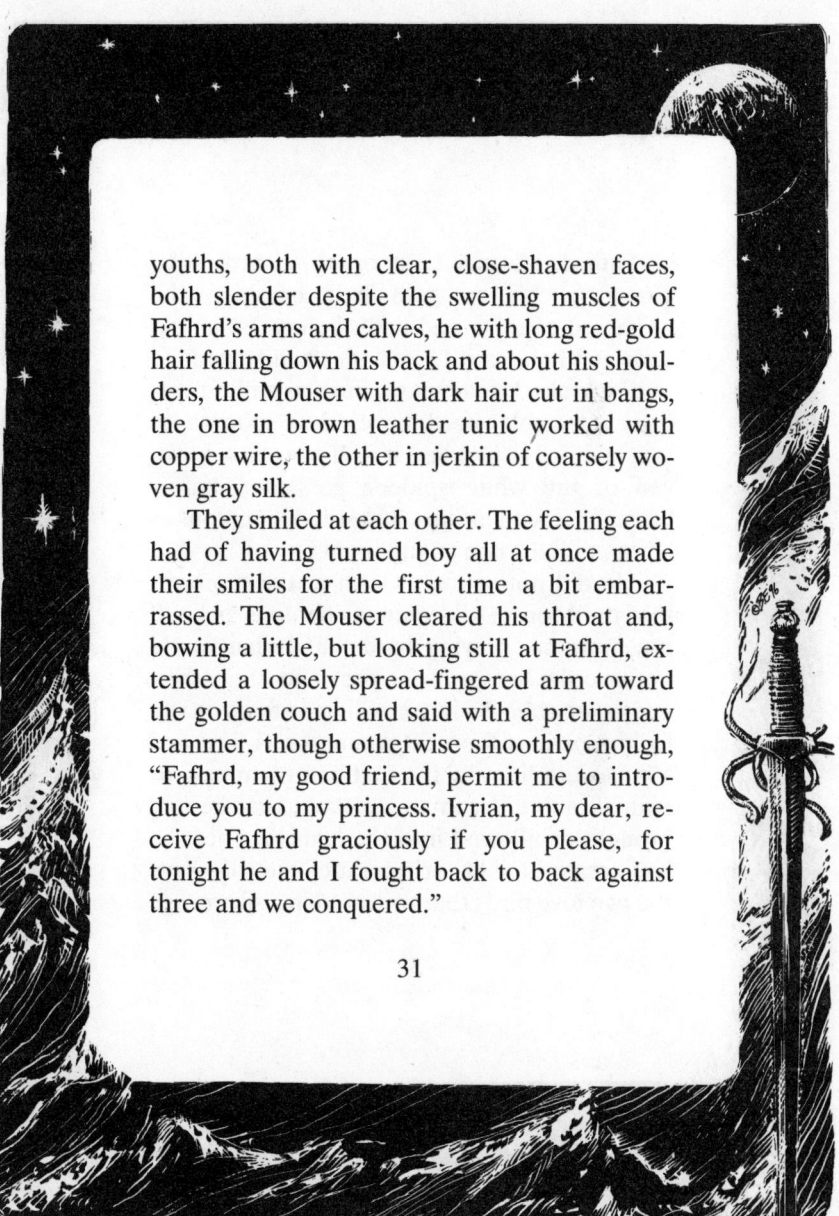

youths, both with clear, close-shaven faces, both slender despite the swelling muscles of Fafhrd's arms and calves, he with long red-gold hair falling down his back and about his shoulders, the Mouser with dark hair cut in bangs, the one in brown leather tunic worked with copper wire, the other in jerkin of coarsely woven gray silk.

They smiled at each other. The feeling each had of having turned boy all at once made their smiles for the first time a bit embarrassed. The Mouser cleared his throat and, bowing a little, but looking still at Fafhrd, extended a loosely spread-fingered arm toward the golden couch and said with a preliminary stammer, though otherwise smoothly enough, "Fafhrd, my good friend, permit me to introduce you to my princess. Ivrian, my dear, receive Fafhrd graciously if you please, for tonight he and I fought back to back against three and we conquered."

Fafhrd advanced, stooping a little, the crown of his red-gold hair brushing the bestarred canopy, and knelt before Ivrian exactly as Vlana had. The slender hand extended to him looked steady now, but was still quiveringly a-tremble, he discovered as soon as he touched it. He handled it as if it were silk woven of the white spider's gossamer, barely brushing it with his lips, and still felt nervous as he mumbled some compliments.

He did not sense, at least at the moment, that the Mouser was quite as nervous as he, if not more so, praying hard that Ivrian would not overdo her princess part and snub their guests, or collapse in trembling or tears or run to him or into the next room, for Fafhrd and Vlana were literally the first beings, human or animal, noble, freeman, or slave, that he had brought or allowed into the luxurious nest he had created for his aristocratic beloved—save the two love birds that twittered in a silver cage hanging to the other side of the fireplace from the dais.

Despite his shrewdness and new-found cynicism it never occurred to the Mouser that it was chiefly his charming but preposterous coddling of Ivrian that was keeping doll-like and even making more so the potentially brave and realistic girl who had fled with him from her father's torture chamber four moons ago.

But now as Ivrian smiled at last and Fafhrd gently returned her hand and cautiously backed off, the Mouser relaxed with relief, fetched two silver cups and two silver mugs, wiped them needlessly with a silken towel, carefully selected a bottle of violet wine, then with a grin at Fafhrd uncorked instead one of the jugs the Northerner had brought, and near-brimmed the four gleaming vessels and served them all four. With another preliminary clearing of throat, but no trace of stammer this time, he toasted, "To my greatest theft to date in Lankhmar, which willy-nilly I must share sixty-sixty with"—he couldn't resist the sudden impulse—"with this great, longhaired, barbarian lout here!" And he downed a quarter of his mug of pleasantly burning wine fortified with brandy.

Fafhrd quaffed off half of his, then toasted back, "To the most boastful and finical little civilized chap I've ever deigned to share loot with," quaffed off the rest, and with a great smile that showed white teeth held out his empty mug.

The Mouser gave him a refill, topped off his own, then set that down to go to Ivrian and pour into her lap from their small pouch the gems he'd filched from Fissif. They gleamed in their new, enviable location like a small puddle of rainbow-hued quicksilver.

Ivrian jerked back a-tremble, almost spilling them, but Vlana gently caught her arm, steadying it, and leaned in over the jewels with

a throaty gasp of wonder and admiration, slowly turned an envious gaze on the pale girl, and began rather urgently but smilingly to whisper to her. Fafhrd realized that Vlana was acting now, but acting well and effectively, since Ivrian was soon nodding eagerly and not long after that beginning to whisper back. At her direction, Vlana fetched a blue-enameled box inlaid with silver, and the two of them transferred the jewels from Ivrian's lap into its blue velvet interior. Then Ivrian placed the box close beside her and they chatted on.

As he worked through his second mug in smaller gulps, Fafhrd relaxed and began to get a deeper feeling of his surroundings. The dazzling wonder of the first glimpse of this throne room in a slum, its colorful luxury intensified by contrast with the dark and mud and slime and rotten stairs and Ordure Boulevard just outside, faded, and he began to note the rickettiness and rot under the grand overlay.

Black, rotten wood and dry, cracked wood too showed here and there between the drapes and also loosed their sick, ancient stinks. The whole floor sagged under the rugs, as much as a span at the center of the room. A large cockroach was climbing down a gold-worked drape, another toward the couch. Threads of night-smog were coming through the shutters, making evanescent black arabesques against the gilt. The stones of the large fireplace had been scrubbed and varnished, yet most of the mortar was gone from between them; some sagged, others were missing altogether.

The Mouser had been building a fire there in the stove. Now he pushed in all the way the yellow flaring kindler he'd lit from the fire-pot, hooked the little black door shut over the mounting flames, and turned back into the room. As if he'd read Fafhrd's mind, he took up several cones of incense, set their peaks

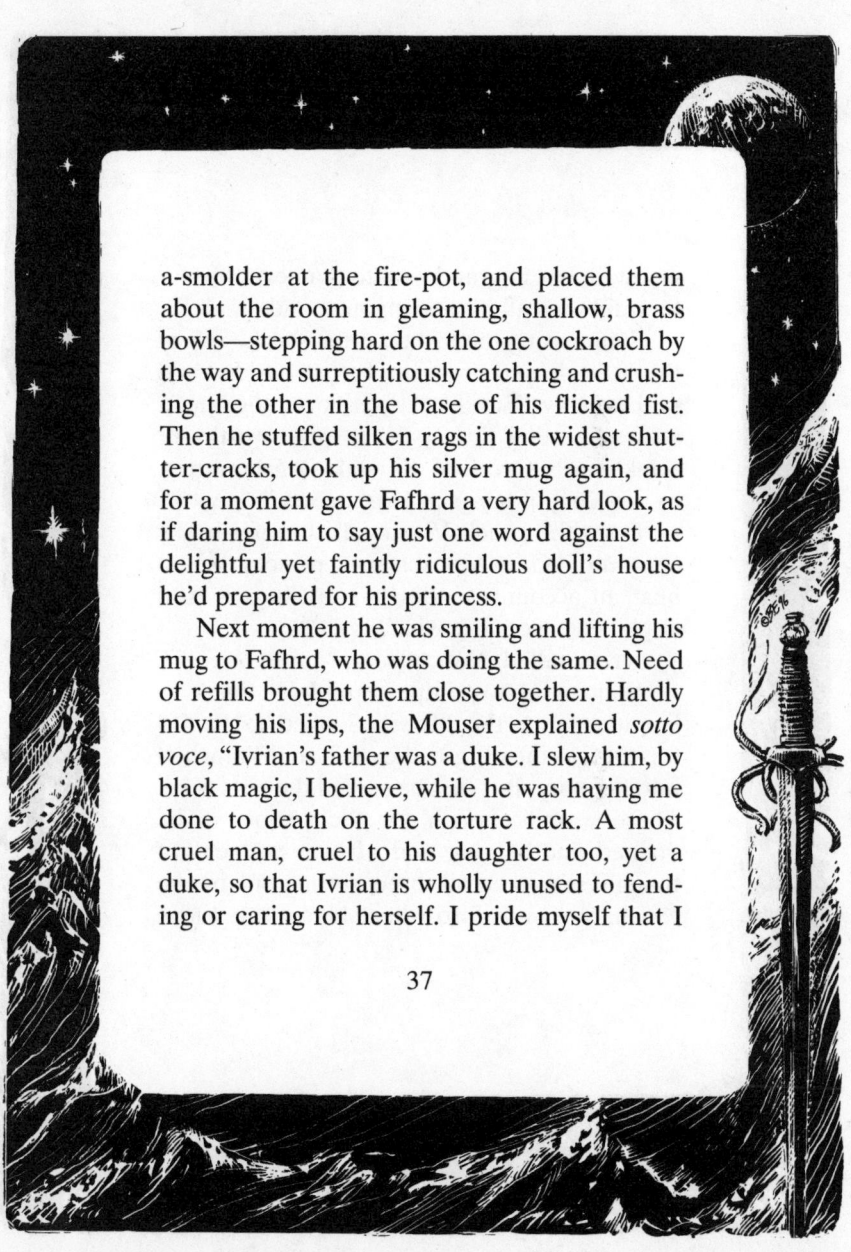

a-smolder at the fire-pot, and placed them about the room in gleaming, shallow, brass bowls—stepping hard on the one cockroach by the way and surreptitiously catching and crushing the other in the base of his flicked fist. Then he stuffed silken rags in the widest shutter-cracks, took up his silver mug again, and for a moment gave Fafhrd a very hard look, as if daring him to say just one word against the delightful yet faintly ridiculous doll's house he'd prepared for his princess.

Next moment he was smiling and lifting his mug to Fafhrd, who was doing the same. Need of refills brought them close together. Hardly moving his lips, the Mouser explained *sotto voce*, "Ivrian's father was a duke. I slew him, by black magic, I believe, while he was having me done to death on the torture rack. A most cruel man, cruel to his daughter too, yet a duke, so that Ivrian is wholly unused to fending or caring for herself. I pride myself that I

maintain her in grander state than ever her father did with all his serving men and maids."

Suppressing the instant criticisms he felt of this attitude and program, Fafhrd nodded and said amiably, "Surely you've thieved together a most charming little palace, quite worthy of Lankhmar's Overlord Karstak Ovartamortes, or the King of Kings at Horborixen."

From the couch Vlana called in her husky contralto, "Gray Mouser, your princess would hear an account of tonight's adventure. And might we have more wine?"

Ivrian called, "Yes, please, Mouse."

Wincing almost imperceptibly at that earlier nickname, the Mouser looked to Fafhrd for the go-ahead, got the nod, and launched into his story. But first he served the girls wine. There wasn't enough for their cups, so he opened another jug and after a moment of thought uncorked all three, setting one by the couch, one by Fafhrd where he sprawled now on the pillowy carpets, and reserving one for himself. Ivrian looked wide-eyed apprehensive at this signal of heavy drinking ahead, Vlana cynical with a touch of anger, but neither voiced their criticism.

The Mouser told the tale of counter-thievery well, acting it out in part, and with only the most artistic of embellishments—the ferret-marmoset before escaping ran up his back and tried to scratch out his eyes—and he was interrupted only twice.

When he said, "And so with a whish and a snick I bared Scalpel—" Fafhrd remarked, "Oh, so you've nicknamed your sword as well as yourself?"

The Mouser drew himself up. "Yes, and I call my dirk Cat's Claw. Any objections? Seem childish to you?"

"Not at all. I call my own sword Graywand. All weapons are in a fashion alive, civilized and nameworthy. Pray continue."

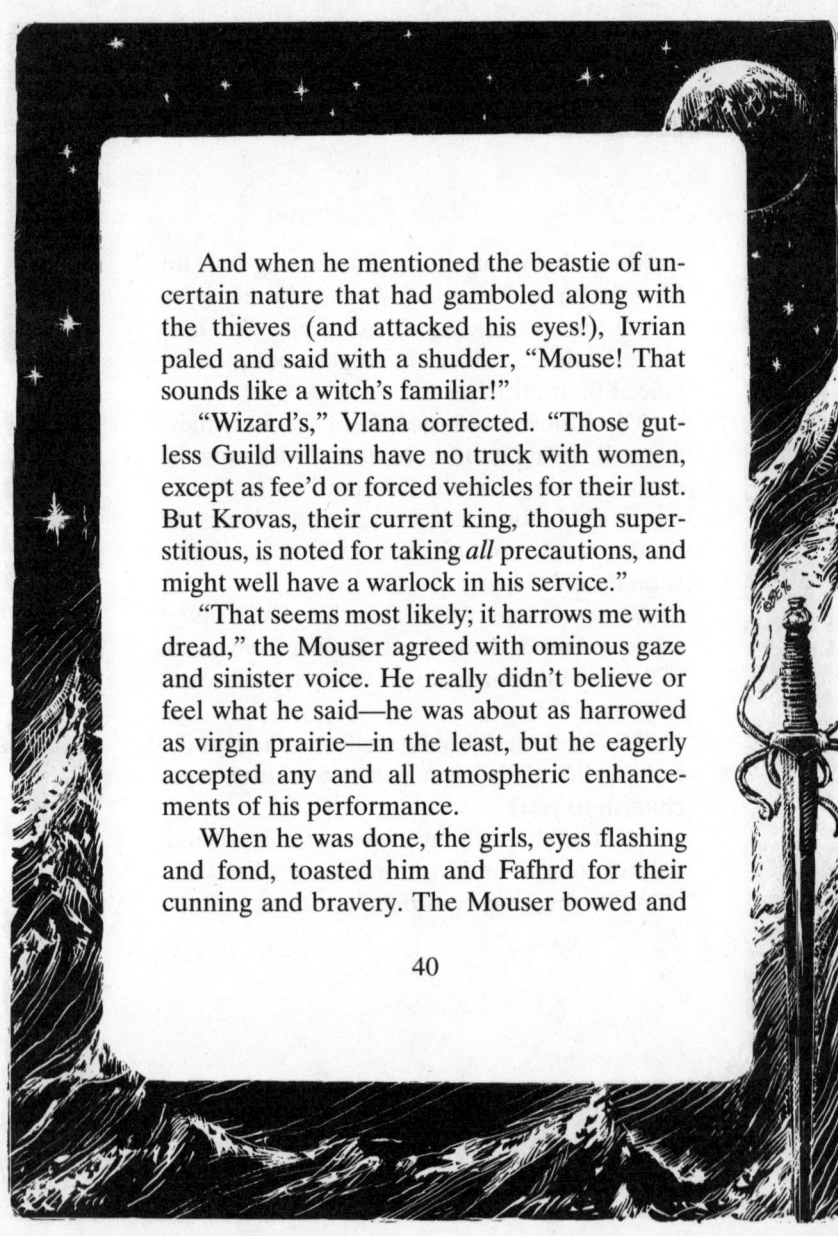

And when he mentioned the beastie of uncertain nature that had gamboled along with the thieves (and attacked his eyes!), Ivrian paled and said with a shudder, "Mouse! That sounds like a witch's familiar!"

"Wizard's," Vlana corrected. "Those gutless Guild villains have no truck with women, except as fee'd or forced vehicles for their lust. But Krovas, their current king, though superstitious, is noted for taking *all* precautions, and might well have a warlock in his service."

"That seems most likely; it harrows me with dread," the Mouser agreed with ominous gaze and sinister voice. He really didn't believe or feel what he said—he was about as harrowed as virgin prairie—in the least, but he eagerly accepted any and all atmospheric enhancements of his performance.

When he was done, the girls, eyes flashing and fond, toasted him and Fafhrd for their cunning and bravery. The Mouser bowed and

eye-twinklingly smiled about, then sprawled him down with a weary sigh, wiping his forehead with a silken cloth and downing a large drink.

After asking Vlana's leave, Fafhrd told the adventurous tale of their escape from Cold Corner—he from his clan, she from an acting troupe—and of their progress to Lankhmar, where they lodged now in an actors' tenement near the Plaza of Dark Delights. Ivrian hugged herself to Vlana and shivered large-eyed at the witchy parts—at least as much in delight as fear of Fafhrd's tale, he thought. He told himself it was natural that a doll-girl should love ghost stories, though he wondered if her pleasure would have been as great if she had known that his ghost stories were truly true. She seemed to live in worlds of imagination—once more at least half the Mouser's doing, he was sure.

The only proper matter he omitted from his

account was Vlana's fixed intent to get a monstrous revenge on the Thieves' Guild for torturing to death her accomplices and harrying her out of Lankhmar when she'd tried freelance thieving in the city, with miming as a cover. Nor of course did he mention his own promise—foolish, he thought now—to help her in this bloody business.

After he'd done and got his applause, he found his throat dry despite his skald's training, but when he sought to wet it, he discovered that his mug was empty and his jug too, though he didn't feel in the least drunk; he had talked all the liquor out of him, he told himself, a little of the stuff escaping in each glowing word he'd spoken.

The Mouser was in like plight and not drunk either—though inclined to pause mysteriously and peer toward infinity before answering question or making remark. This time he suggested, after a particularly long infinity-gaze, that Fafhrd accompany him to the Eel while he purchased a fresh supply.

"But we've a lot of wine left in *our* jug," Ivrian protested. "Or at least a little," she amended. It did sound empty when Vlana shook it. "Besides, you've wine of all sorts here."

"Not this sort, dearest, and first rule is never mix 'em," the Mouser explained, wagging a finger. "That way lies unhealth, aye, and madness."

"My dear," Vlana said, sympathetically patting Ivrian's wrist, "at some time in any good party all the men who are really men simply have to go out. It's extremely stupid, but it's their nature and can't be dodged, believe me."

"But, Mouse, I'm scared. Fafhrd's tale frightened me. So did yours—I'll hear that big-headed, black, ratty familiar a-scratch at the shutters when you're gone, I know I will!"

It seemed to Fafhrd she was not afraid at

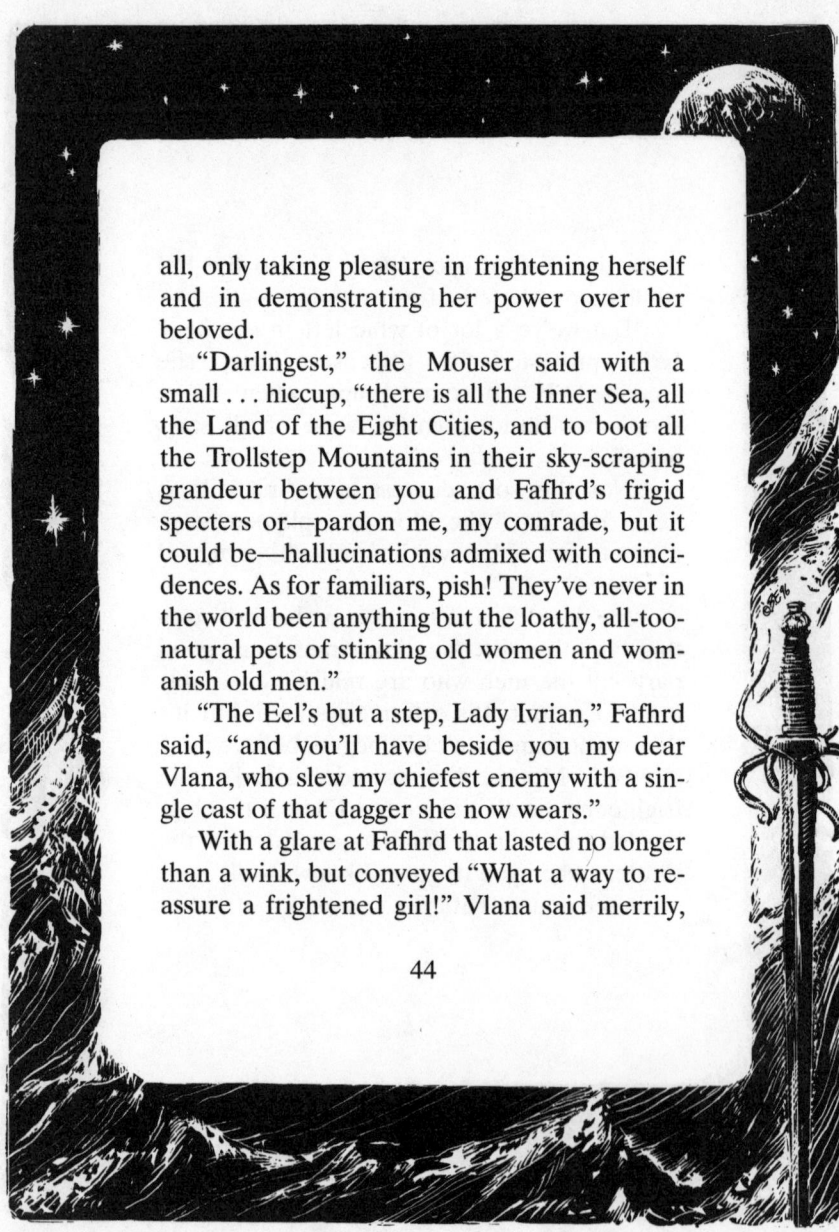

all, only taking pleasure in frightening herself and in demonstrating her power over her beloved.

"Darlingest," the Mouser said with a small . . . hiccup, "there is all the Inner Sea, all the Land of the Eight Cities, and to boot all the Trollstep Mountains in their sky-scraping grandeur between you and Fafhrd's frigid specters or—pardon me, my comrade, but it could be—hallucinations admixed with coincidences. As for familiars, pish! They've never in the world been anything but the loathy, all-too-natural pets of stinking old women and womanish old men."

"The Eel's but a step, Lady Ivrian," Fafhrd said, "and you'll have beside you my dear Vlana, who slew my chiefest enemy with a single cast of that dagger she now wears."

With a glare at Fafhrd that lasted no longer than a wink, but conveyed "What a way to reassure a frightened girl!" Vlana said merrily,

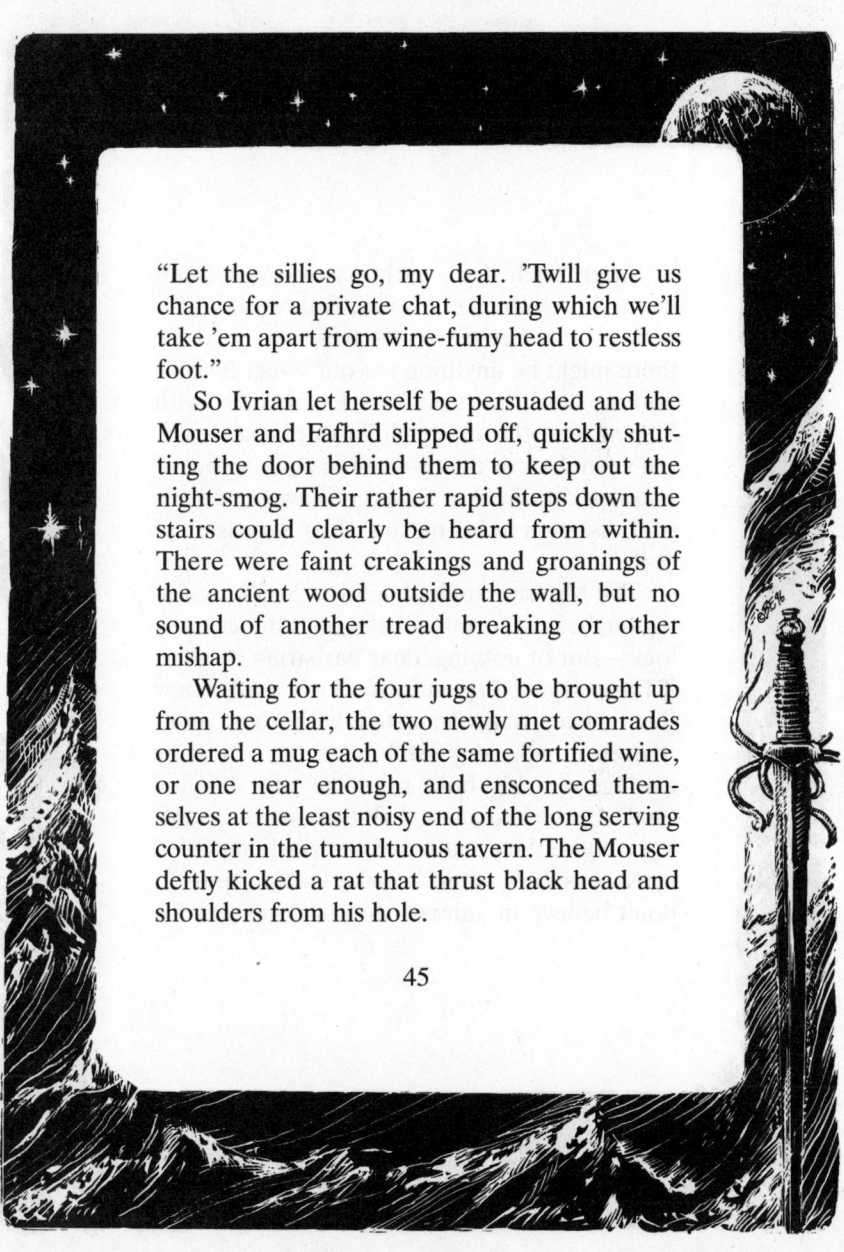

"Let the sillies go, my dear. 'Twill give us chance for a private chat, during which we'll take 'em apart from wine-fumy head to restless foot."

So Ivrian let herself be persuaded and the Mouser and Fafhrd slipped off, quickly shutting the door behind them to keep out the night-smog. Their rather rapid steps down the stairs could clearly be heard from within. There were faint creakings and groanings of the ancient wood outside the wall, but no sound of another tread breaking or other mishap.

Waiting for the four jugs to be brought up from the cellar, the two newly met comrades ordered a mug each of the same fortified wine, or one near enough, and ensconced themselves at the least noisy end of the long serving counter in the tumultuous tavern. The Mouser deftly kicked a rat that thrust black head and shoulders from his hole.

After each had enthusiastically complimented the other on his girl, Fafhrd said diffidently, "Just between ourselves, do you think there might be anything to your sweet Ivrian's notion that the small dark creature with Slivikin and the other Guild-thief was a wizard's familiar, or at any rate the cunning pet of a sorcerer, trained to act as go-between and report disasters to his master or to Krovas or to both?"

The Mouser laughed lightly. "You're building bugbears—formless baby ones unlicked by logic—out of nothing, dear barbarian brother, if I may say so. *Imprimis*, we don't really know the beastie was connected with the Guild-thieves at all. May well have been a stray catling or a big bold rat—like this damned one!" He kicked again. "But, *secundus*, granting it to be the creature of a wizard employed by Krovas, how could it make useful report? I don't believe in animals that talk—except for

parrots and such birds, which only . . . parrot—or ones having an elaborate sign language men can share. Or perhaps you envisage the beastie dipping its paddy paw in a jug of ink and writing its report in big on a floor-spread parchment?

"Ho, there, you back of the counter! Where are my jugs? Rats eaten the boy who went for them days ago? Or he simply starved to death while on his cellar quest? Well, tell him to get a swifter move on and meanwhile brim us again!

"No, Fafhrd, even granting the beastie to be directly or indirectly a creature of Krovas, and that it raced back to Thieves' House after our affray, what could it tell them there? Only that something had gone wrong with the burglary at Jengao's. Which they'd soon suspect in any case from the delay in the thieves' and bravos' return."

Fafhrd frowned and muttered stubbornly,

"The furry slinker might, nevertheless, convey our appearances to the Guild masters, and they might recognize us and come after us and attack us in our homes. Or Slivikin and his fat pal, revived from their bumps, might do likewise."

"My dear friend," the Mouser said condolingly, "once more begging your indulgence, I fear this potent wine is addling your wits. If the Guild knew our looks or where we lodge, they'd have been nastily on our necks days, weeks, nay, months ago. Or conceivably you don't know that their penalty for freelance or even unassigned thieving within the walls of Lankhmar and for three leagues outside them is nothing less than death, after torture if happily that can be achieved."

"I know all about that and my plight is worse even than yours," Fafhrd retorted, and after pledging the Mouser to secrecy told him the tale of Vlana's vendetta against the Guild

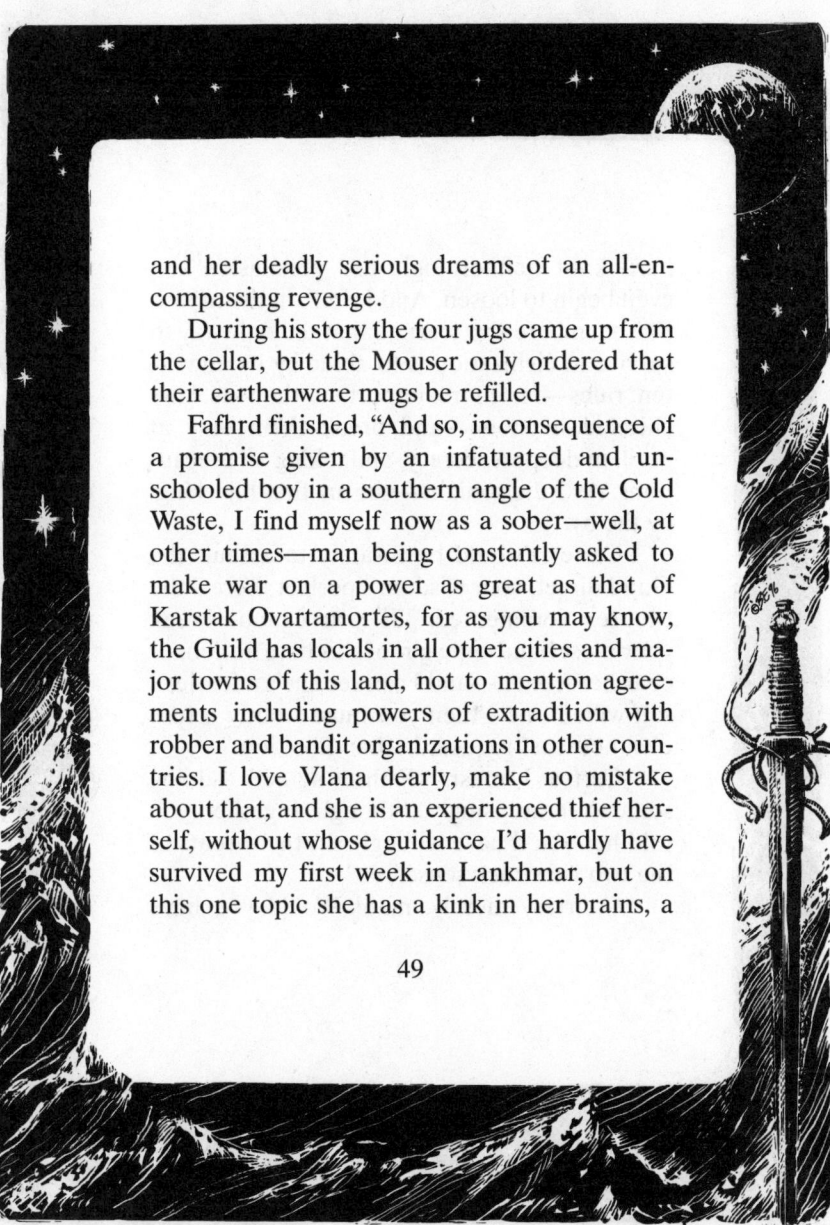

and her deadly serious dreams of an all-encompassing revenge.

During his story the four jugs came up from the cellar, but the Mouser only ordered that their earthenware mugs be refilled.

Fafhrd finished, "And so, in consequence of a promise given by an infatuated and unschooled boy in a southern angle of the Cold Waste, I find myself now as a sober—well, at other times—man being constantly asked to make war on a power as great as that of Karstak Ovartamortes, for as you may know, the Guild has locals in all other cities and major towns of this land, not to mention agreements including powers of extradition with robber and bandit organizations in other countries. I love Vlana dearly, make no mistake about that, and she is an experienced thief herself, without whose guidance I'd hardly have survived my first week in Lankhmar, but on this one topic she has a kink in her brains, a hard knot neither logic nor persuasion can even begin to loosen. And I, well, in the month I've been here I've learned that the only way to survive in civilization is to abide by its unwritten rules—far more important than its laws chiseled in stone—and break them only at peril, in deepest secrecy, and taking all precautions. As I did tonight—not my first hijacking, by the by."

"Certes t'would be insanity to assault the Guild direct, your wisdom's perfect there," the Mouser commented. "If you cannot break your most handsome girl of this mad notion, or coax her from it—and I can see she's a fearless, self-willed one—then you must stoutly refuse e'en her least request in that direction."

"Certes I must," Fafhrd agreed, adding somewhat accusingly, "though I gather you told her you'd have willingly slit the throats of the two we struck senseless."

"Courtesy merely, man! Would you have

had me behave ungraciously to your girl? 'Tis measure of the value I was already setting then on your goodwill. But only a woman's man may cross her. As you must, in this instance."

"Certes I must," Fafhrd repeated with great emphasis and conviction. "I'd be an idiot taking on the Guild. Of course if they should catch me they'd kill me in any case for freelancing and highjacking. But wantonly to assault the Guild direct, kill one Guild-thief needlessly, only behave as if I might—lunacy entire!"

"You'd not only be a drunken, drooling idiot, you'd questionless be stinking in three nights at most from that emperor of diseases, Death. Malicious attacks on her person, blows directed at the organization, the Guild requites tenfold what she does other rule-breakings. All planned robberies and other thefts would be called off and the entire power of the Guild and its allies mobilized against you alone. I'd count your chances better to take on single-handed the host of the King of Kings rather than the Thieves' Guild's subtle minions. In view of your size, might, and wit you're a squad perhaps, or even a company, but hardly an army. So, no least giving-in to Vlana in this one matter."

"Agreed!" Fafhrd said loudly, shaking the Mouser's iron-thewed hand in a near crusher grip.

"And now we should be getting back to the girls," the Mouser said.

"After one more drink while we settle the score. Ho, boy!"

"Suits." The Mouser dug into his pouch to pay, but Fafhrd protested vehemently. In the end they tossed coin for it, and Fafhrd won and with great satisfaction clinked out his silver smerduks on the stained and dinted counter also marked with an infinitude of mug circles, as if it had been once the desk of a mad

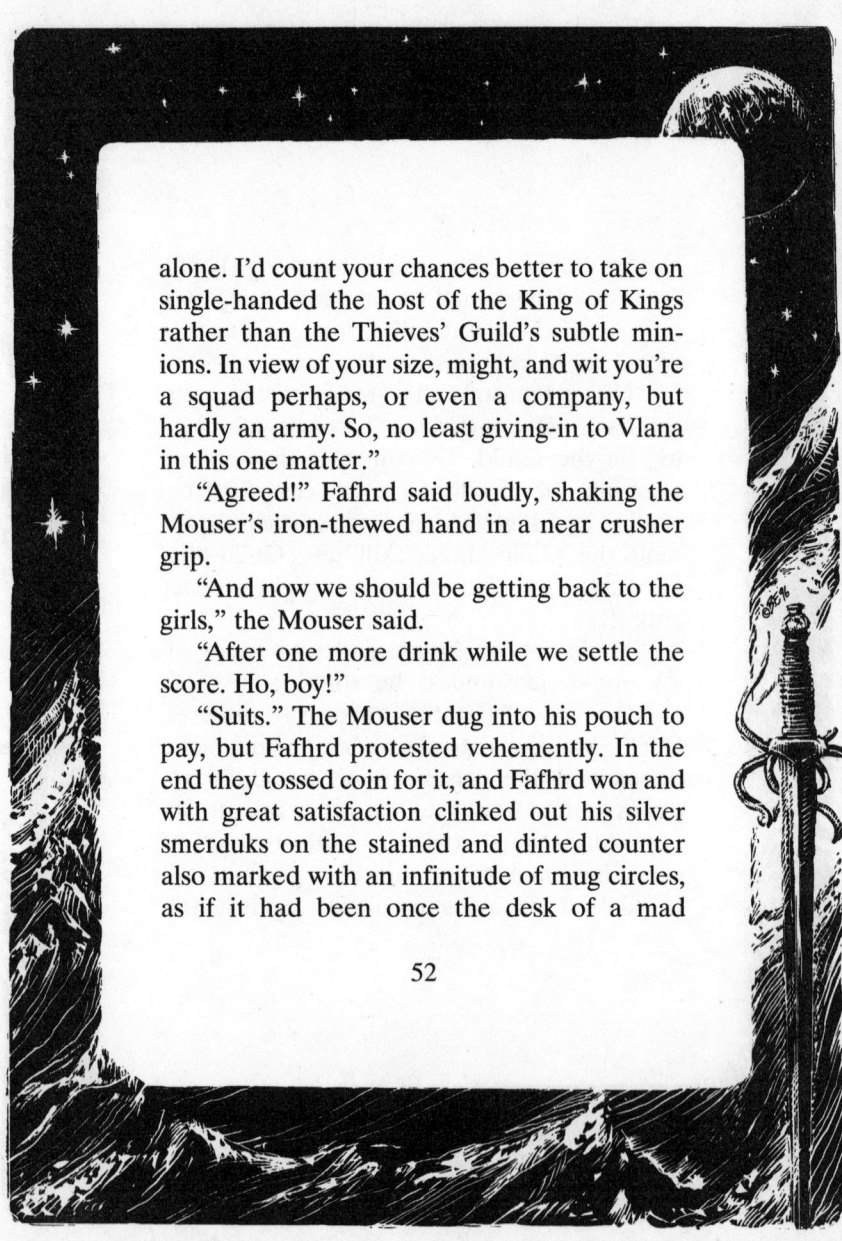

geometer. They pushed themselves to their feet, the Mouser giving the rathole one last light kick for luck.

At this, Fafhrd's thoughts looped back and he said, "Grant the beastie can't paw-write, or talk by mouth or paw, it still could have followed us at distance, marked down your dwelling, and then returned to Thieves' House to lead its masters down on us like a hound!"

"Now you're speaking shrewd sense again," the Mouser said. "Ho, boy, a bucket of small beer to go! On the instant!" Noting Fafhrd's blank look, he explained, "I'll spill it outside the Eel to kill our scent and all the way down the passageway. Yes, and splash it high on the walls too."

Fafhrd nodded wisely. "I thought I'd drunk my way past the addled point."

Vlana and Ivrian, deep in excited talk, both started at the pounding rush of footsteps up the stairs. Racing behemoths could hardly have made more noise. The creaking and groaning were prodigious and there were the crashes of two treads breaking, yet the pounding footsteps never faltered. The door flew open and their two men rushed in through a great mushroom top of night-smog which was neatly sliced off its black stem by the slam of the door.

"I told you we'd be back in a wink," the Mouser cried gayly to Ivrian, while Fafhrd strode forward, unmindful of the creaking floor, crying, "Dearest heart, I've missed you sorely," and caught up Vlana despite her voiced protests and pushings-off and kissed and hugged her soundly before setting her back on the couch again.

Oddly, it was Ivrian who appeared to be angry at Fafhrd then, rather than Vlana, who was smiling fondly if somewhat dazedly.

"Fafhrd, sir," she said boldly, little fists set on her narrow hips, her tapered chin held high,

her dark eyes blazing, "my beloved Vlana has been telling me about the unspeakably atrocious things the Thieves' Guild did to her and to her dearest friends. Pardon my frank speaking to one I've only met, but I think it quite unmanly of you to refuse her the just revenge she desires and fully deserves. And that goes for you too, Mouse, who boasted to Vlana of what you would have done had you but known, who in like case did not scruple to slay my very own father—or reputed father—for his cruelties!"

It was clear to Fafhrd that while he and the Gray Mouser had idly boozed in the Eel, Vlana had been giving Ivrian a doubtless empurpled account of her grievances against the Guild and playing mercilessly on the naive girl's bookish, romantic sympathies and high concept of knightly honor. It was also clear to him that Ivrian was more than a little drunk. A three-quarters empty flask of violet wine of far Kiraay sat on the low table next to them.

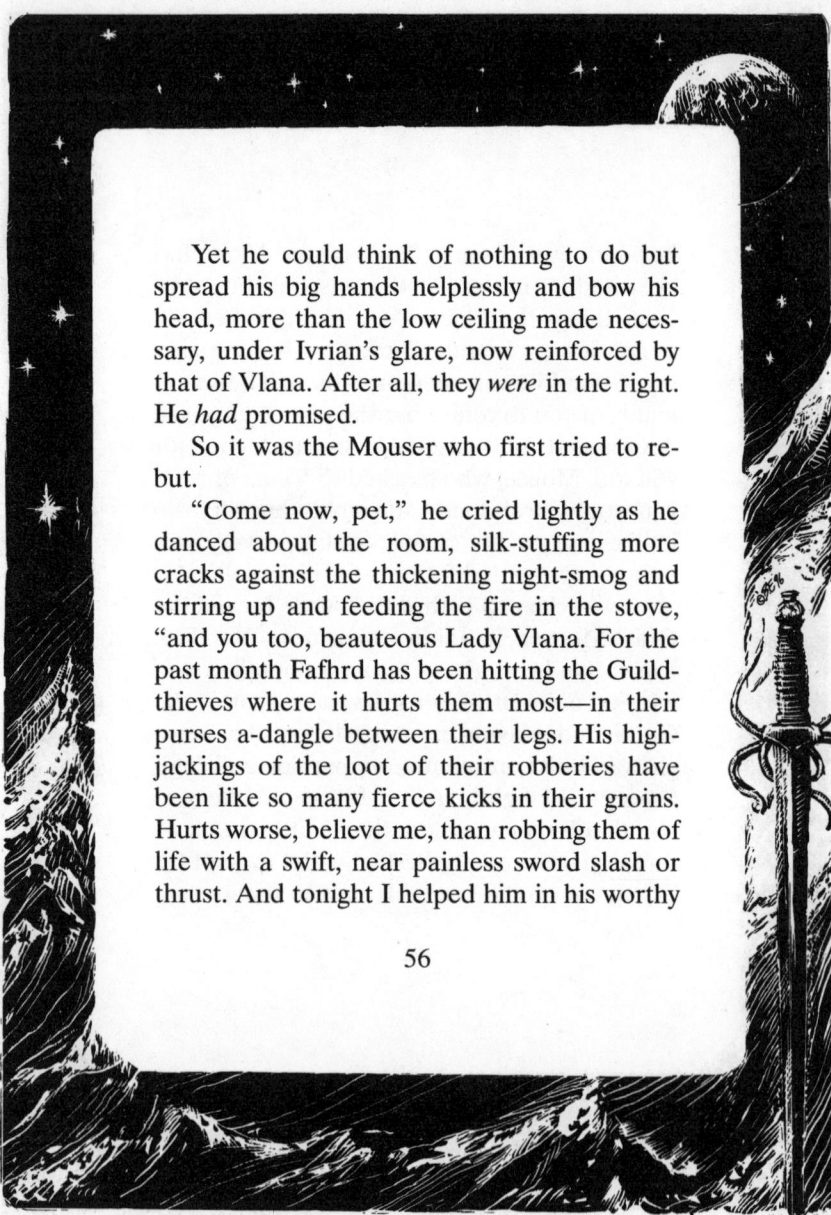

Yet he could think of nothing to do but spread his big hands helplessly and bow his head, more than the low ceiling made necessary, under Ivrian's glare, now reinforced by that of Vlana. After all, they *were* in the right. He *had* promised.

So it was the Mouser who first tried to rebut.

"Come now, pet," he cried lightly as he danced about the room, silk-stuffing more cracks against the thickening night-smog and stirring up and feeding the fire in the stove, "and you too, beauteous Lady Vlana. For the past month Fafhrd has been hitting the Guild-thieves where it hurts them most—in their purses a-dangle between their legs. His high-jackings of the loot of their robberies have been like so many fierce kicks in their groins. Hurts worse, believe me, than robbing them of life with a swift, near painless sword slash or thrust. And tonight I helped him in his worthy purpose—and will eagerly do so again. Come, drink we up all." Under his handling, one of the new jugs came uncorked with a pop and he darted about brimming silver cups and mugs.

"A merchant's revenge!" Ivrian retorted with scorn, not one whit appeased, but rather angered anew. "Ye both are at heart true and gentle knights, I know, despite all current backsliding. At the least you must bring Vlana the head of Krovas!"

"What would she *do* with it? What *good* would it be except to spot the carpets?" the Mouser plaintively inquired, while Fafhrd, gathering his wits at last and going down on one knee, said slowly, "Most respected Lady Ivrian, it is true I solemnly promised my beloved Vlana I would help her in her revenge, but that was while I was still in barbarous Cold Corner, where blood-feud is a commonplace, sanctioned by custom and accepted by all the clans and tribes and brotherhoods of the sav-

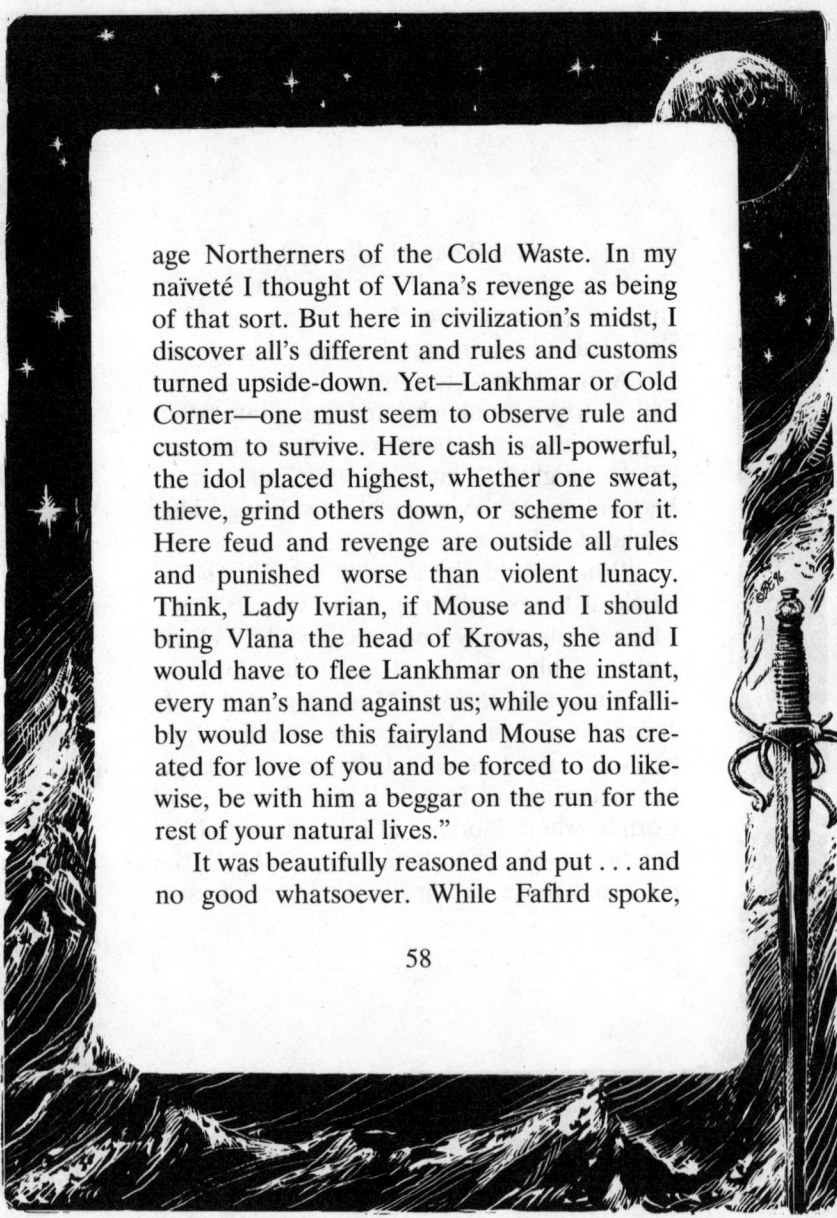

age Northerners of the Cold Waste. In my naïveté I thought of Vlana's revenge as being of that sort. But here in civilization's midst, I discover all's different and rules and customs turned upside-down. Yet—Lankhmar or Cold Corner—one must seem to observe rule and custom to survive. Here cash is all-powerful, the idol placed highest, whether one sweat, thieve, grind others down, or scheme for it. Here feud and revenge are outside all rules and punished worse than violent lunacy. Think, Lady Ivrian, if Mouse and I should bring Vlana the head of Krovas, she and I would have to flee Lankhmar on the instant, every man's hand against us; while you infallibly would lose this fairyland Mouse has created for love of you and be forced to do likewise, be with him a beggar on the run for the rest of your natural lives."

It was beautifully reasoned and put . . . and no good whatsoever. While Fafhrd spoke,

Ivrian snatched up her new-filled cup and drained it. Now she stood up straight as a soldier, her pale face flushed, and said scathingly to Fafhrd kneeling before her, *"You count the cost!* You speak to me of *things"*—she waved at the many-hued splendor around her—"of mere property, however costly, when *honor* is at stake. You gave Vlana *your word.* Oh, is knighthood wholly dead? And that applies to you, too, Mouse, who swore you'd slit the miserable throats of two noisome Guild-thieves."

"I didn't swear *to*," the Mouser objected feebly, downing a big drink. "I merely said I *would have*," while Fafhrd could only shrug again and writhe inside and gulp a little easement from his silver mug. For Ivrian was speaking in the same guilt-showering tones and using the same unfair yet heart-cleaving womanly arguments as Mor his mother might have, or Mara, his deserted Snow Clan sweetheart and avowed wife, big-bellied by now with his child.

In a master stroke, Vlana tried gently to draw Ivrian down to her golden seat again. "Softly, dearest," she pleaded. "You have spoken nobly for me and my cause, and believe me, I am most grateful. Your words revived in me great, fine feelings dead these many years. But of us here, only you are truly an aristocrat attuned to the highest proprieties. We other three are naught but thieves. Is it any wonder some of us put safety above honor and word-keeping, and most prudently avoid risking our lives? Yes, we are three thieves and I am outvoted. So please speak no more of honor and rash, dauntless bravery, but sit you down and—"

"You mean they're both *afraid* to challenge the Thieves' Guild, don't you?" Ivrian said, eyes wide and face twisted by loathing. "I always thought my Mouse was a nobleman first

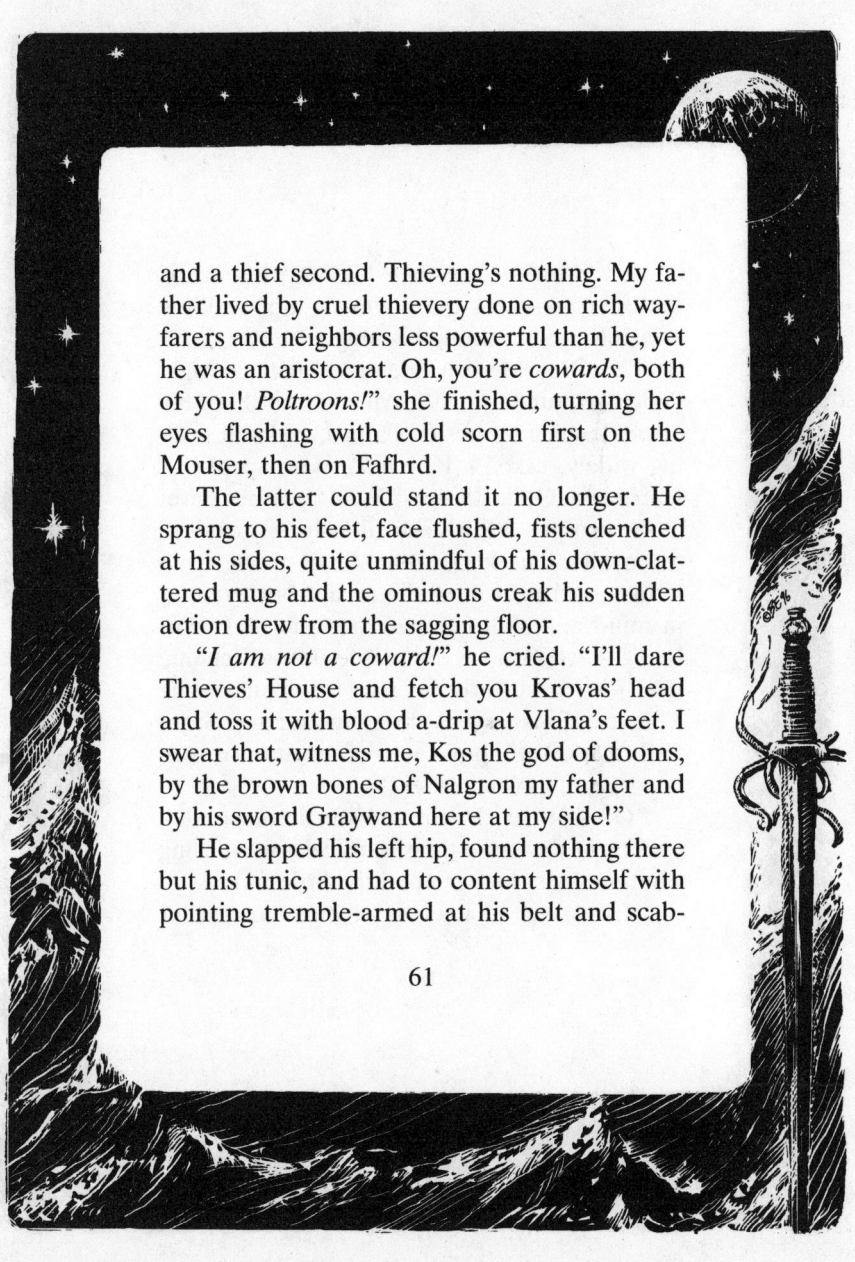

and a thief second. Thieving's nothing. My father lived by cruel thievery done on rich wayfarers and neighbors less powerful than he, yet he was an aristocrat. Oh, you're *cowards*, both of you! *Poltroons!*" she finished, turning her eyes flashing with cold scorn first on the Mouser, then on Fafhrd.

The latter could stand it no longer. He sprang to his feet, face flushed, fists clenched at his sides, quite unmindful of his down-clattered mug and the ominous creak his sudden action drew from the sagging floor.

"*I am not a coward!*" he cried. "I'll dare Thieves' House and fetch you Krovas' head and toss it with blood a-drip at Vlana's feet. I swear that, witness me, Kos the god of dooms, by the brown bones of Nalgron my father and by his sword Graywand here at my side!"

He slapped his left hip, found nothing there but his tunic, and had to content himself with pointing tremble-armed at his belt and scabbarded sword where they lay atop his neatly folded robe—and then picking up, refilling splashily, and draining his mug.

The Gray Mouser began to laugh in high, delighted, tuneful peals. All stared at him. He came dancing up beside Fafhrd, and still smiling widely, asked, "*Why not?* Who speaks of fearing the Guild-thieves? Who becomes upset at the prospect of this ridiculously easy exploit, when all of us know that all of them, even Krovas and his ruling clique, are but pygmies in mind and skill compared to me or Fafhrd here? A wondrously simple, foolproof scheme has just occurred to me for penetrating Thieves' House, every closet and cranny. Stout Fafhrd and I will put it into effect at once. Are you with me, Northerner?"

"Of course I am," Fafhrd responded gruffly, at the same time frantically wondering what madness had gripped the little fellow.

"Give me a few heartbeats to gather

needed props, and we're off!" the Mouser cried. He snatched from a shelf and unfolded a stout sack, then raced about, thrusting into it coiled ropes, bandage rolls, rags, jars of ointment and unction and unguent, and other oddments.

"But you can't go *tonight*," Ivrian protested, suddenly grown pale and uncertain-voiced. "You're both . . . in no condition to."

"You're both *drunk*," Vlana said harshly. "Silly drunk—and that way you'll get naught in Thieves' House but your deaths. Fafhrd, where's that heartless reason you employed to slay or ice-veined see slain a clutch of mighty rivals and win me at Cold Corner and in the chilly, sorcery-webbed depths of Trollstep Canyon? Revive it! And infuse some into your skipping gray friend."

"Oh, no," Fafhrd told her as he buckled on his sword. "You wanted the head of Krovas heaved at your feet in a great splatter of blood, and that's what you're going to get, like it or not!"

"Softly, Fafhrd," the Mouser interjected, coming to a sudden stop and drawing tight the sack's mouth by its strings. "And softly you too, Lady Vlana, and my dear princess. Tonight I intend but a scouting expedition. No risks run, only the information gained needful for planning our murderous strike tomorrow or the day after. So no head-choppings whatsoever tonight, Fafhrd, you hear me? Whatever mayhap, hist's the word. And don your hooded robe."

Fafhrd shrugged, nodded, and obeyed.

Ivrian seemed somewhat relieved. Vlana too, though she said, "Just the same you're both drunk."

"All to the good!" the Mouser assured her with a mad smile. "Drink may slow a man's sword-arm and soften his blows a bit, but it sets his wits ablaze and fires his imagination, and

those are the qualities we'll need tonight. Besides," he hurried on, cutting off some doubt Ivrian was about to voice, "drunken men are supremely cautious! Have you ever seen a staggering sot pull himself together at sight of the guard and walk circumspectly and softly past?"

"Yes," Vlana said, "and fall flat on his face just as he comes abreast 'em."

"Pish!" the Mouser retorted and, throwing back his head, grandly walked toward her along an imaginary straight line. Instantly he tripped over his own foot, plunged forward, suddenly without touching floor did an incredible forward flip, heels over head, and landed erect and quite softly—toes, ankles, and knees bending just at the right moment to soak up impact—directly in front of the girls. The floor barely complained.

"You see?" he said, straightening up and unexpectedly reeling backward. He tripped over the pillow on which lay his cloak and sword, but by a wrenching twist and a lurch stayed upright and began rapidly to accouter himself.

Under cover of this action Fafhrd made quietly yet swiftly to fill once more his and the Mouser's mugs, but Vlana noted it and gave him such a glare that he set down mugs and uncorked jug so swiftly his robe swirled, then stepped back from the drinks table with a shrug of resignation and toward Vlana a grimacing nod.

The Mouser shouldered his sack and drew open the door. With a casual wave at the girls, but no word spoken, Fafhrd stepped out on the tiny porch. The night-smog had grown so thick he was almost lost to view. The Mouser waved four fingers at Ivrian, softly called, "Bye-bye, Misling," then followed Fafhrd.

"Good fortune go with you," Vlana called heartily.

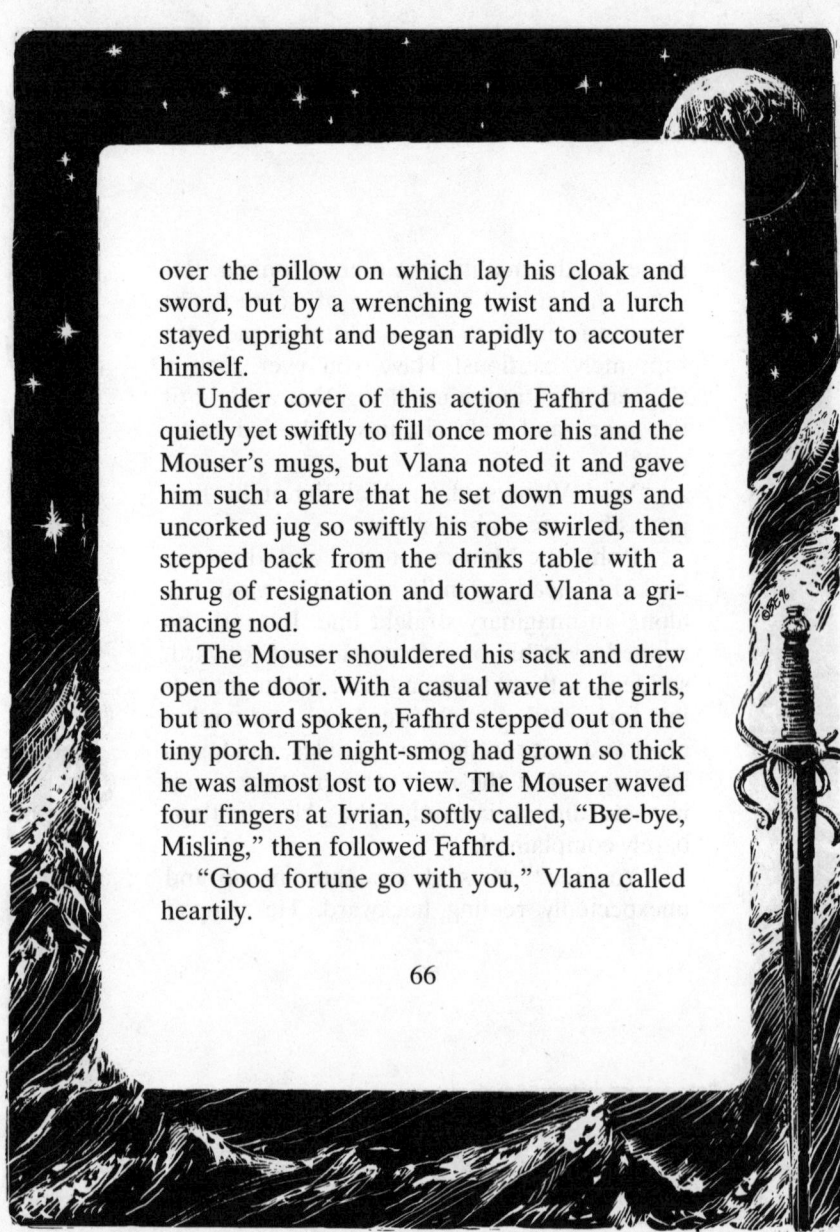

"Oh be careful, Mouse," Ivrian gasped.

The Mouser, his figure slight against the loom of Fafhrd's, silently drew shut the door.

Their arms automatically gone around each other, the girls waited for the inevitable creaking and groaning of the stairs. It delayed and delayed. The night-smog that had entered the room dissipated and still the silence was unbroken. "What can they be doing out there?" Ivrian whispered. "Plotting their course?"

Vlana, scowling, impatiently shook her head, then disentangled herself, tiptoed to the door, opened it, descended softly a few steps, which creaked most dolefully, then returned, shutting the door behind her.

"They're gone," she said in wonder, her eyes wide, her hands spread a little to either side, palms up.

"I'm frightened!" Ivrian breathed and sped across the room to embrace the taller girl.

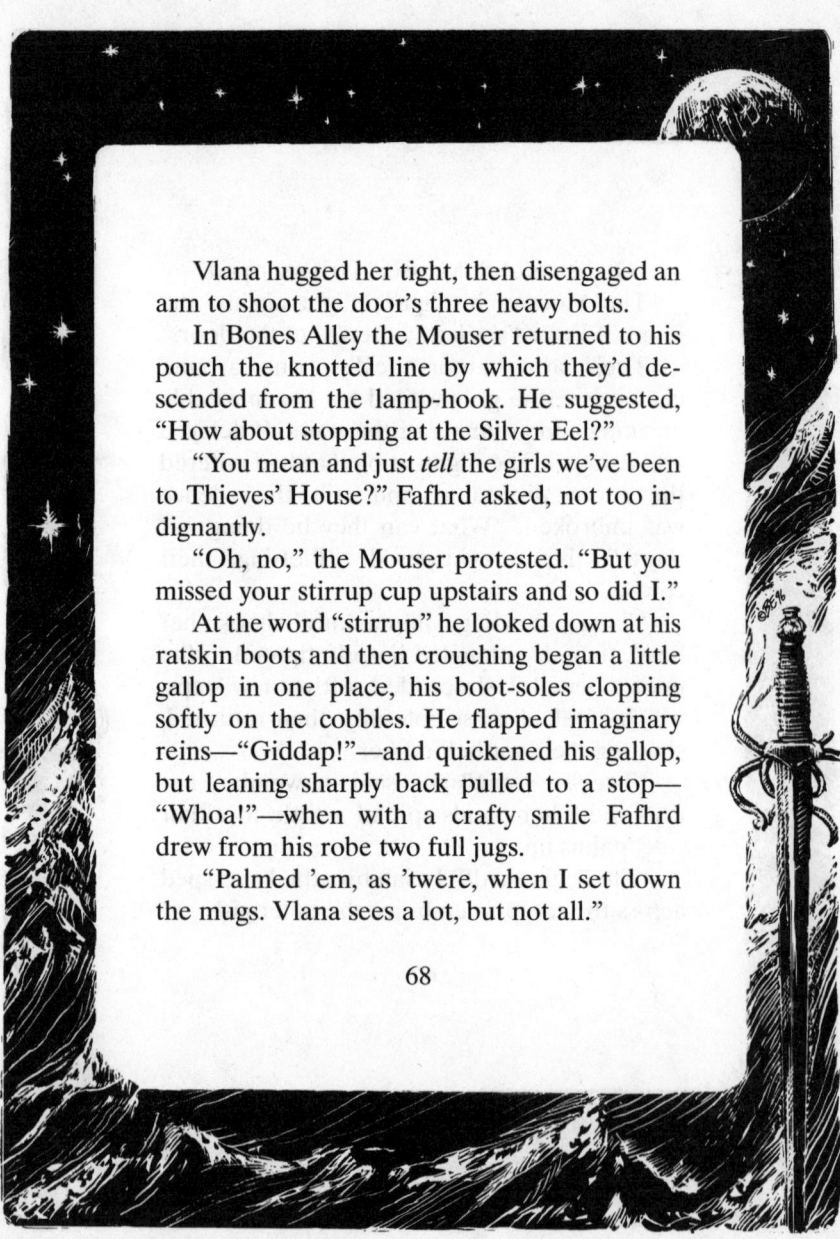

Vlana hugged her tight, then disengaged an arm to shoot the door's three heavy bolts.

In Bones Alley the Mouser returned to his pouch the knotted line by which they'd descended from the lamp-hook. He suggested, "How about stopping at the Silver Eel?"

"You mean and just *tell* the girls we've been to Thieves' House?" Fafhrd asked, not too indignantly.

"Oh, no," the Mouser protested. "But you missed your stirrup cup upstairs and so did I."

At the word "stirrup" he looked down at his ratskin boots and then crouching began a little gallop in one place, his boot-soles clopping softly on the cobbles. He flapped imaginary reins—"Giddap!"—and quickened his gallop, but leaning sharply back pulled to a stop—"Whoa!"—when with a crafty smile Fafhrd drew from his robe two full jugs.

"Palmed 'em, as 'twere, when I set down the mugs. Vlana sees a lot, but not all."

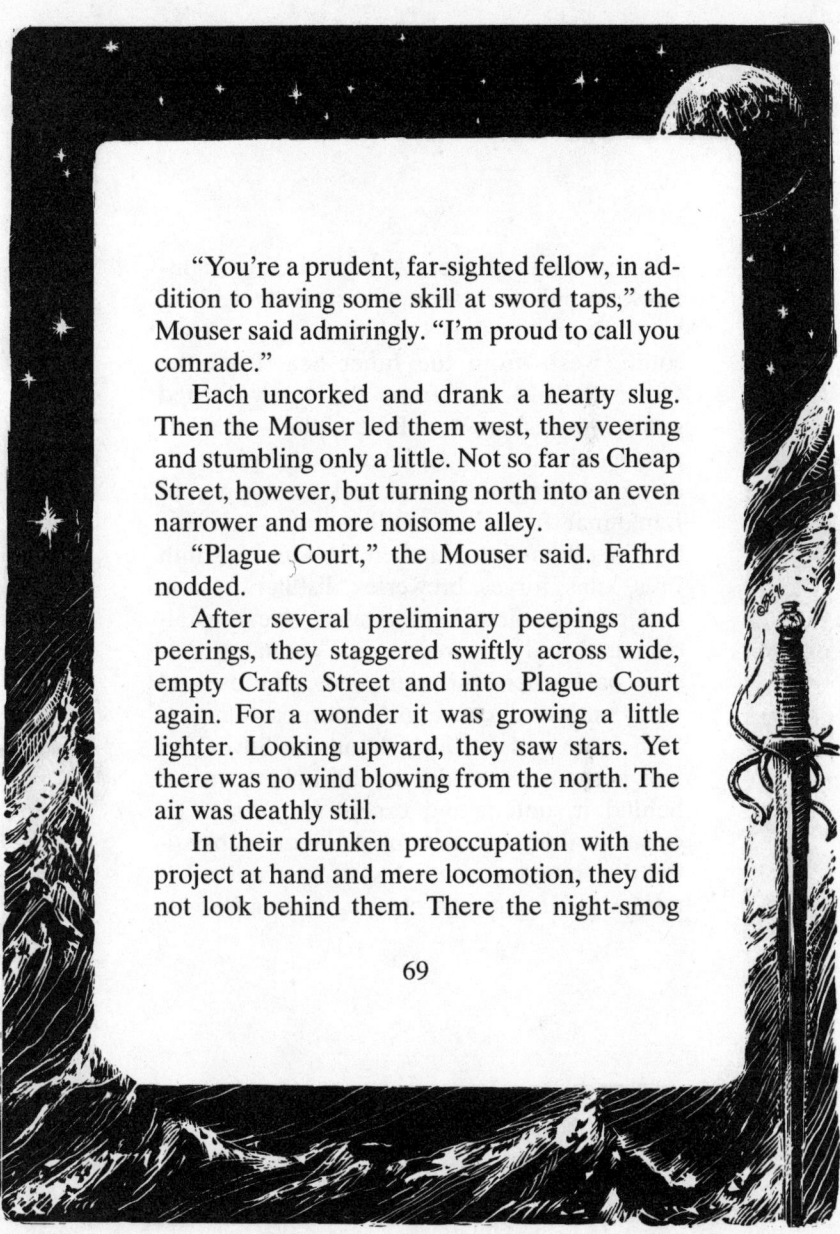

"You're a prudent, far-sighted fellow, in addition to having some skill at sword taps," the Mouser said admiringly. "I'm proud to call you comrade."

Each uncorked and drank a hearty slug. Then the Mouser led them west, they veering and stumbling only a little. Not so far as Cheap Street, however, but turning north into an even narrower and more noisome alley.

"Plague Court," the Mouser said. Fafhrd nodded.

After several preliminary peepings and peerings, they staggered swiftly across wide, empty Crafts Street and into Plague Court again. For a wonder it was growing a little lighter. Looking upward, they saw stars. Yet there was no wind blowing from the north. The air was deathly still.

In their drunken preoccupation with the project at hand and mere locomotion, they did not look behind them. There the night-smog was thicker than ever. A high-circling nighthawk would have seen the stuff converging from all sections of Lankhmar, north, east, south, west—from the Inner Sea, from the Great Salt Marsh, from the many-ditched grain lands, from the River Hlal—in swift-moving black rivers and rivulets, heaping, eddying, swirling, dark and reeking essence of Lankhmar from its branding irons, braziers, bonfires, bonefires, kitchen fires and warmth fires, kilns, forges, breweries, distilleries, junk and garbage fires innumerable, sweating alchemists' and sorcerers' dens, crematoriums, charcoal burners' turfed mounds, all those and many more ... converging purposefully on Dim Lane and particularly on the Silver Eel and perhaps especially on the ricketty house behind it, untenanted except for attic. The closer to that center it got, the more substantial the smog became, eddy-strands and swirl-tatters tearing off and clinging to rough stone corners and scraggly-surfaced brick like black cobwebs.

But the Mouser and Fafhrd merely exclaimed in mild, muted amazement at the stars, muggily mused as to how much the improved visibility would increase the risk of their quest, and cautiously crossing the Street of the Thinkers, called Atheist Avenue by moralists, continued to Plague Court until it forked.

The Mouser chose the left branch, which trended northwest.

"Death Alley."

Fafhrd nodded.

After a curve and recurve, Cheap Street swung into sight about thirty paces ahead. The Mouser stopped at once and lightly threw his arm against Fafhrd's chest.

Clearly in view across Cheap Street was a wide, low, open doorway, framed by grimy stone blocks. There led up to it two steps hol-

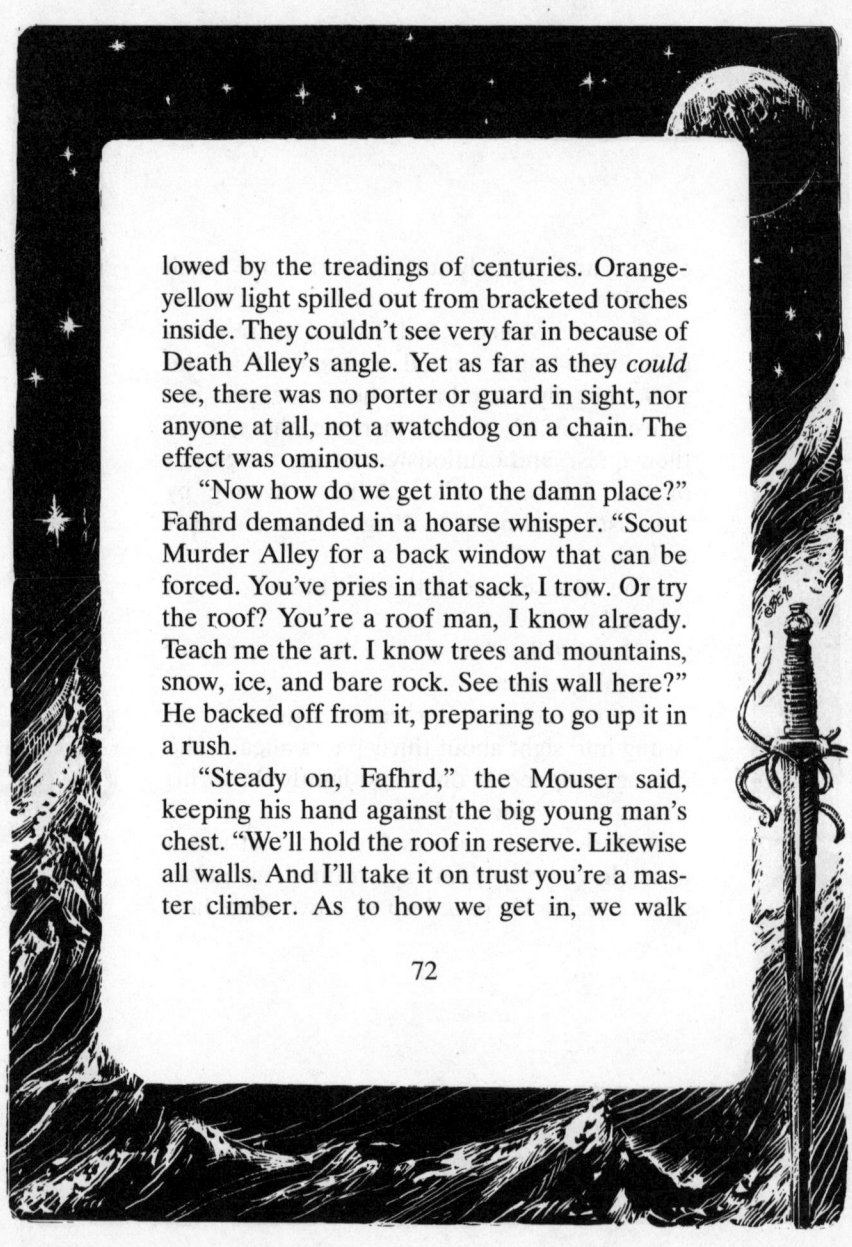

lowed by the treadings of centuries. Orange-yellow light spilled out from bracketed torches inside. They couldn't see very far in because of Death Alley's angle. Yet as far as they *could* see, there was no porter or guard in sight, nor anyone at all, not a watchdog on a chain. The effect was ominous.

"Now how do we get into the damn place?" Fafhrd demanded in a hoarse whisper. "Scout Murder Alley for a back window that can be forced. You've pries in that sack, I trow. Or try the roof? You're a roof man, I know already. Teach me the art. I know trees and mountains, snow, ice, and bare rock. See this wall here?" He backed off from it, preparing to go up it in a rush.

"Steady on, Fafhrd," the Mouser said, keeping his hand against the big young man's chest. "We'll hold the roof in reserve. Likewise all walls. And I'll take it on trust you're a master climber. As to how we get in, we walk straight through that doorway." He frowned. "Tap and hobble, rather. Come on, while I prepare us."

As he drew the skeptically grimacing Fafhrd back down Death Alley until all Cheap Street was again cut off from view, he explained, "We'll pretend to be beggars, members of *their* guild, which is but a branch of the Thieves' Guild and houses with it, or at any rate reports in to the Beggarmasters at Thieves' House. We'll be new members, who've gone out by day, so it'll not be expected that the Night Beggarmaster and any night watchmen know our looks."

"But we don't look like beggars," Fafhrd protested. "Beggars have awful sores and limbs all a-twist or lacking altogether."

"That's just what I'm going to take care of now," the Mouser chuckled, drawing Scalpel. Ignoring Fafhrd's backward step and wary glance, the Mouser gazed puzzledly at the long

tapering strip of steel he'd bared, then with a happy nod unclipped from his belt Scalpel's scabbard furbished with ratskin, sheathed the sword and swiftly wrapped it up, hilt and all, in a spiral, with the wide ribbon of a bandage roll dug from his sack.

"There!" he said, knotting the bandage ends. "Now I've a tapping cane."

"What's that?" Fafhrd demanded. "And why?"

"Because I'll be blind, that's why." He took a few shuffling steps, tapping the cobbles ahead with wrapped sword—gripping it by the quillons, or cross guard, so that the grip and pommel were up his sleeve—and groping ahead with his other hand. "That look all right to you?" he asked Fafhrd as he turned back. "Feels perfect to me. Bat-blind, eh? Oh, don't fret, Fafhrd—the rag's but gauze. I can see through it fairly well. Besides, I don't have to convince anyone inside Thieves' House I'm actually blind. Most Guild-beggars fake it, as you must know. Now what to do with you? Can't have you blind also—too obvious, might wake suspicion." He uncorked his jug and sucked inspiration. Fafhrd copied this action, on principle.

The Mouser smacked his lips and said, "I've got it! Fafhrd, stand on your right leg and double up your left behind you at the knee. Hold! Don't fall on me! Avaunt! But steady yourself by my shoulder. That's right. Now get that left foot higher. We'll disguise your sword like mine, for a crutch cane—it's thicker and'll look just right. You can also steady yourself with your other hand on my shoulder as you hop—the halt leading the blind, always good for a tear, always good theater! But higher with that left foot! No, it just doesn't come off—I'll have to rope it. But first unclip your scabbard."

Soon the Mouser had Graywand and its scabbard in the same state as Scalpel and was

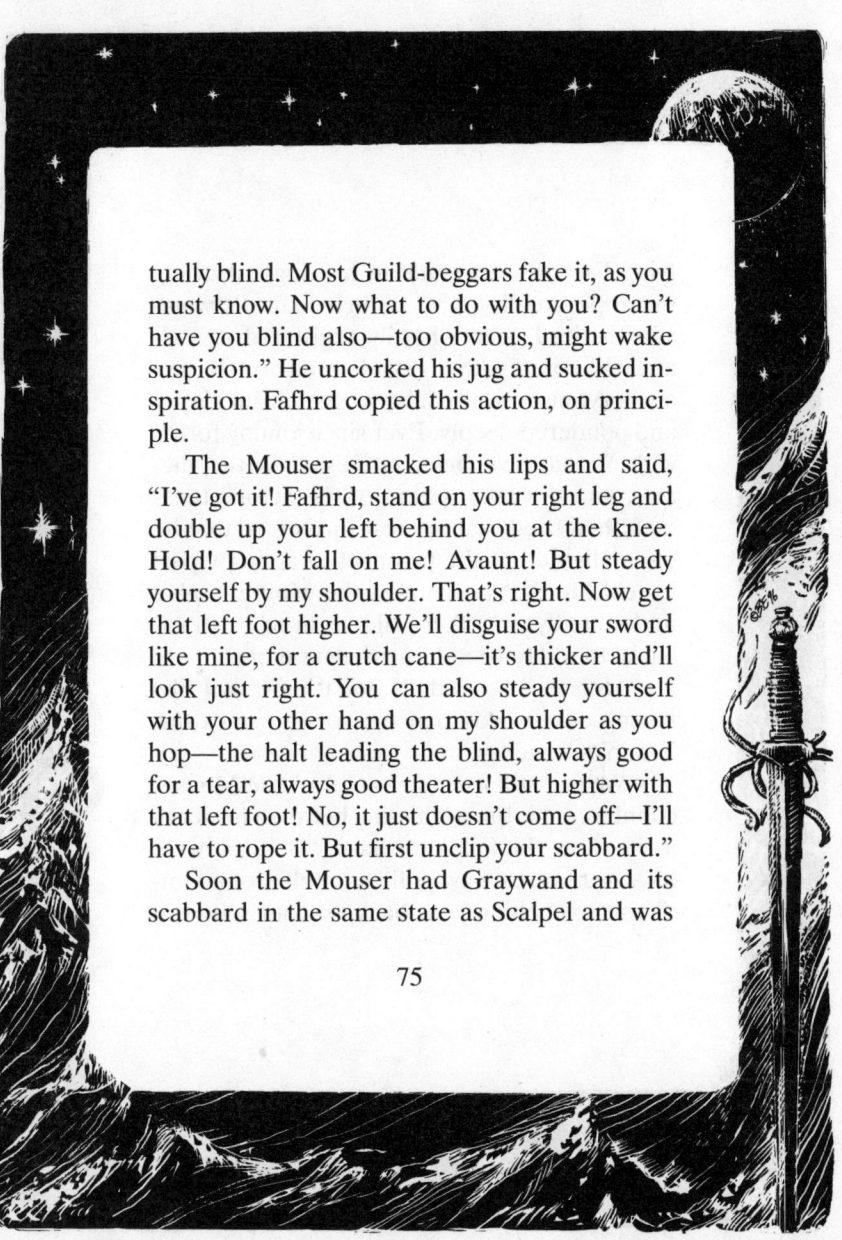

tying Fafhrd's left ankle to his thigh, drawing the rope cruelly tight, though Fafhrd's wine-anesthetized nerves hardly registered it. Balancing himself with his steel-cored crutch cane as the Mouser worked, he swigged from his jug and pondered deeply. Ever since joining forces with Vlana, he'd been interested in the theater, and the atmosphere of the actors' tenement had fired that interest further, so that he was delighted at the prospect of acting a part in real life. Yet brilliant as the Mouser's plan undoubtedly was, there did seem to be drawbacks to it. He tried to formulate them.

"Mouser," he said, "I don't know as I like having our swords tied up, so we can't draw 'em in emergency."

"We can still use 'em as clubs," the Mouser countered, his breath hissing between his teeth as he drew the last knot hard. "Besides, we'll have our knives. Say, pull your belt around until yours is behind your back, so your robe will

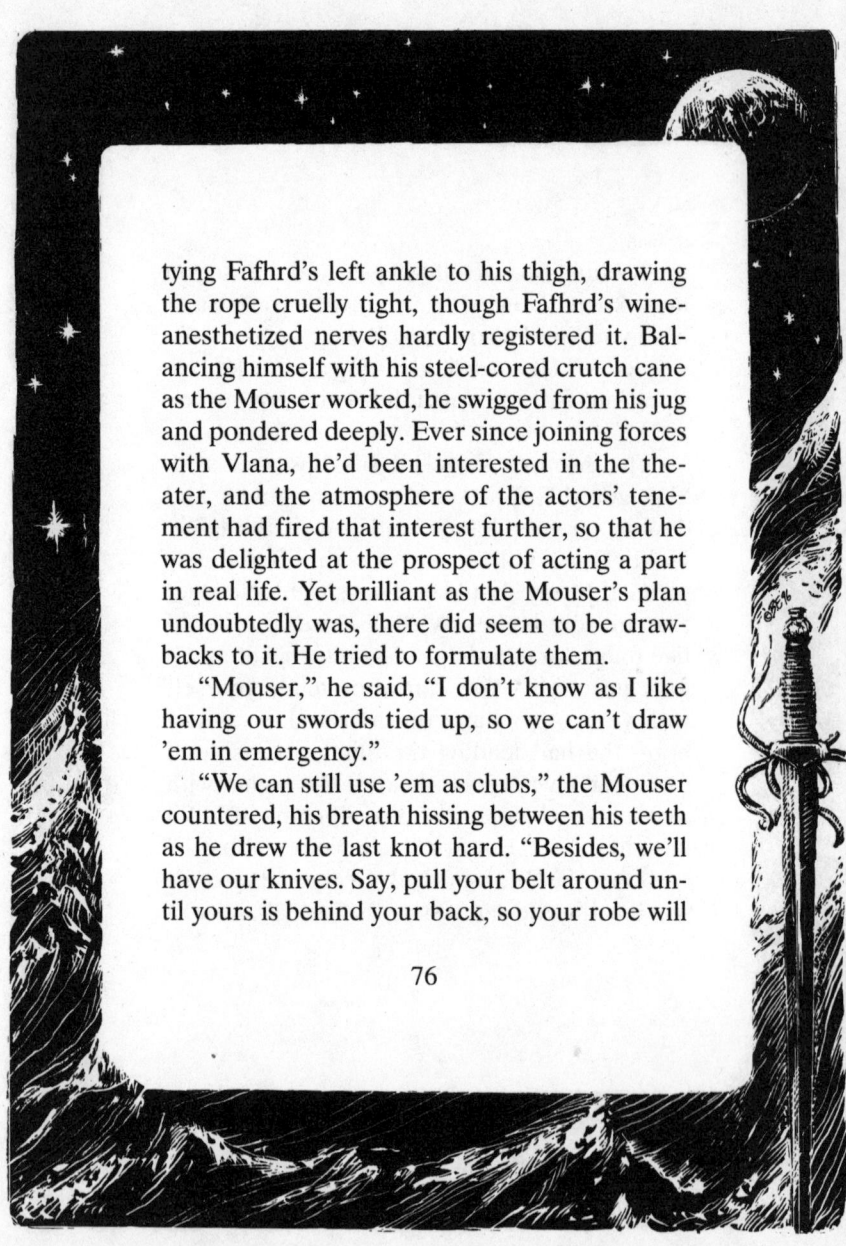

hide it sure. I'll do the same with Cat's Claw. Beggars don't carry weapons, at least in view, and we must maintain dramatic consistency in every detail. Stop drinking now; you've had enough. I myself need only a couple swallows more to reach my finest pitch."

"And I don't know as I like going hobbled into that den of cutthroats. I can hop amazingly fast, it's true, but not as fast as I can run. Is it really wise, think you?"

"You can slash yourself loose in an instant," the Mouser hissed with a touch of impatience and anger. "Aren't you willing to make the least sacrifice for art's sake?"

"Oh, very well," Fafhrd said, draining his jug and tossing it aside. "Yes, of course I am."

"Your complexion's too hale," the Mouser said, inspecting him critically. He touched up Fafhrd's features and hands with pale gray greasepaint, then added wrinkles with dark. "And your garb's too tidy." He scooped dirt

from between the cobbles and smeared it on Fafhrd's robe, then tried to put a rip in it, but the material resisted. He shrugged and tucked his lightened sack under his belt.

"So's yours," Fafhrd observed, and stooping on his right leg got a good handful of muck himself, ordure in it by its feel and stink. Heaving himself up with a mighty effort, he wiped the stuff off on the Mouser's cloak and gray silken jerkin too.

The small man got the odor and cursed, but, "Dramatic consistency," Fafhrd reminded him. "It's well we stink. Beggars do—that's one reason folk give 'em coins: to get rid of 'em. And no one at Thieves' House will be eager to inspect us close. Now come on, while our fires are still high." And grasping hold of the Mouser's shoulder, he propelled himself rapidly toward Cheap Street, setting his bandaged sword between cobbles well ahead and taking mighty hops.

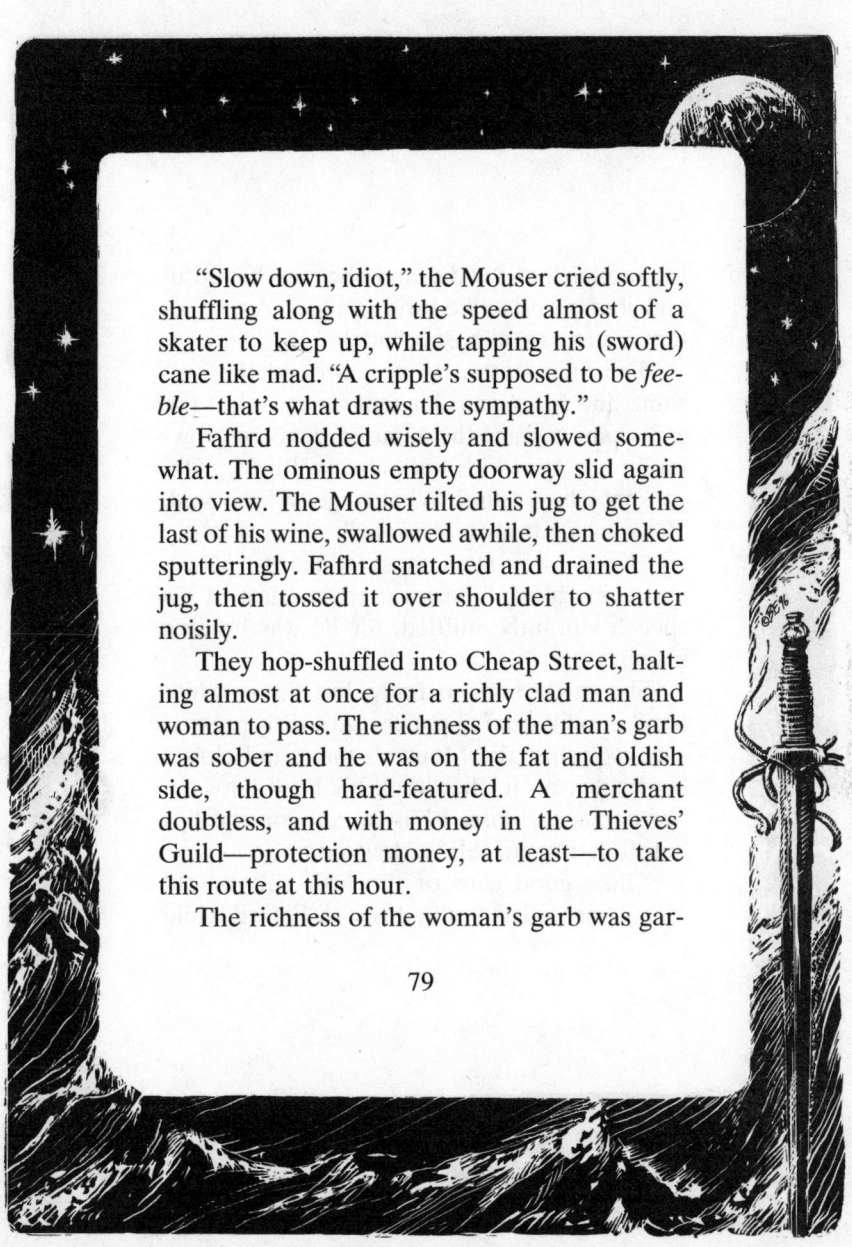

"Slow down, idiot," the Mouser cried softly, shuffling along with the speed almost of a skater to keep up, while tapping his (sword) cane like mad. "A cripple's supposed to be *feeble*—that's what draws the sympathy."

Fafhrd nodded wisely and slowed somewhat. The ominous empty doorway slid again into view. The Mouser tilted his jug to get the last of his wine, swallowed awhile, then choked sputteringly. Fafhrd snatched and drained the jug, then tossed it over shoulder to shatter noisily.

They hop-shuffled into Cheap Street, halting almost at once for a richly clad man and woman to pass. The richness of the man's garb was sober and he was on the fat and oldish side, though hard-featured. A merchant doubtless, and with money in the Thieves' Guild—protection money, at least—to take this route at this hour.

The richness of the woman's garb was garish though not tawdry and she was beautiful and young, and looked still younger. A competent courtesan, almost certainly.

The man started to veer around the noisome and filthy pair, his face averted, but the girl swung toward the Mouser, concern growing in her eyes with hothouse swiftness. "Oh, you poor boy! Blind. What tragedy," she said. "Give us a gift for him, lover."

"Keep away from those stinkards, Misra, and come along," he retorted, the last of his speech vibrantly muffled, for he was holding his nose.

She made him no reply, but thrust white hand into his ermine pouch and swiftly pressed a coin against the Mouser's palm and closed his fingers on it, then took his head between her palms and kissed him sweetly on the lips before letting herself be dragged on.

"Take good care of the little fellow, old man," she called fondly back to Fafhrd while her companion grumbled muffled reproaches at her, of which only "perverted bitch" was intelligible.

The Mouser stared at the coin in his palm, then sneaked a long look after his benefactress. There was a dazed wonder in his voice as he whispered to Fafhrd, "Look. *Gold*. A golden coin and a beautiful woman's sympathy. Think you we should give over this rash project and for a profession take up beggary?"

"Buggery even, rather!" Fafhrd answered harsh and low. That "old man" rankled. "Onward we, bravely!"

They upped the two worn steps and went through the doorway, noting the exceptional thickness of the wall. Ahead was a long, straight, high-ceilinged corridor ending in a stairs and with doors spilling light at intervals and wall-set torches adding their flare, but empty all its length.

They had just got through the doorway

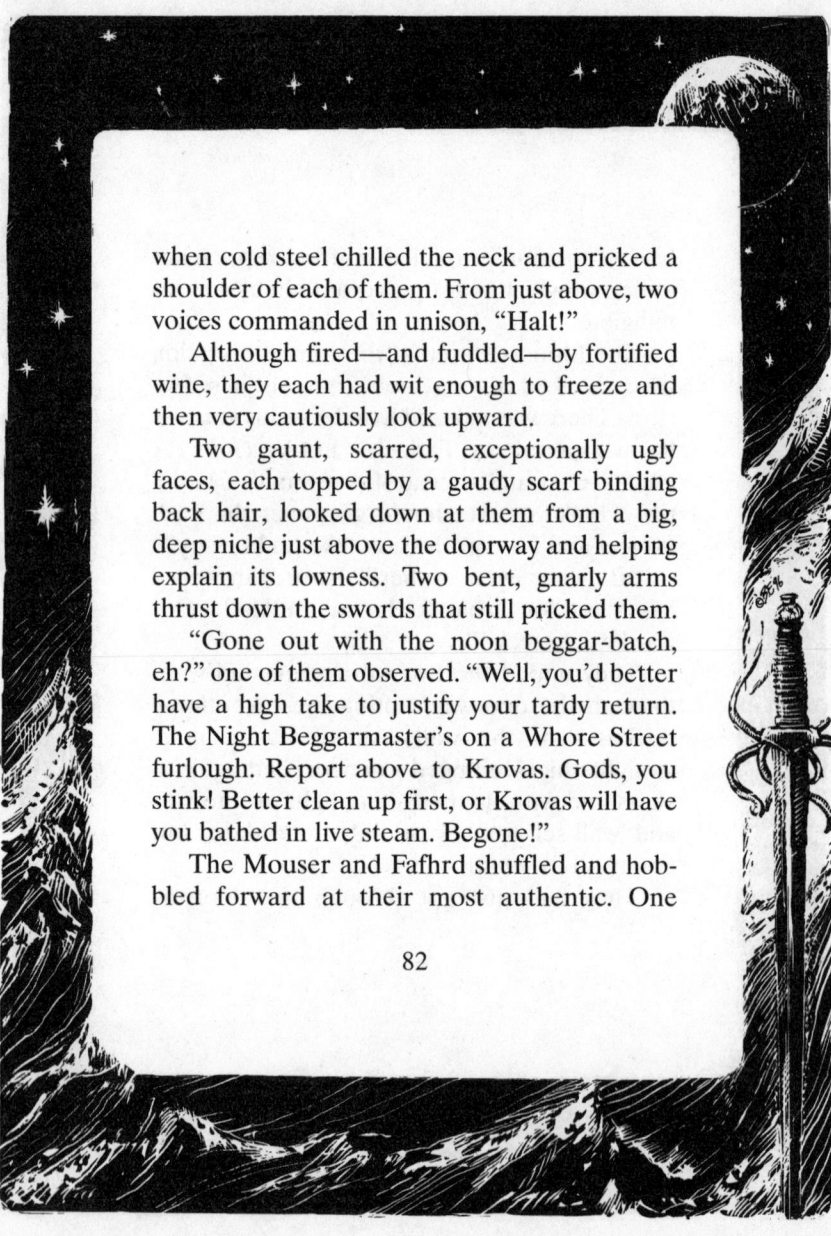

when cold steel chilled the neck and pricked a shoulder of each of them. From just above, two voices commanded in unison, "Halt!"

Although fired—and fuddled—by fortified wine, they each had wit enough to freeze and then very cautiously look upward.

Two gaunt, scarred, exceptionally ugly faces, each topped by a gaudy scarf binding back hair, looked down at them from a big, deep niche just above the doorway and helping explain its lowness. Two bent, gnarly arms thrust down the swords that still pricked them.

"Gone out with the noon beggar-batch, eh?" one of them observed. "Well, you'd better have a high take to justify your tardy return. The Night Beggarmaster's on a Whore Street furlough. Report above to Krovas. Gods, you stink! Better clean up first, or Krovas will have you bathed in live steam. Begone!"

The Mouser and Fafhrd shuffled and hobbled forward at their most authentic. One niche-guard cried after them, "Relax, boys! You don't have to put it on here."

"Practice makes perfect," the Mouser called back in a quavering voice. Fafhrd's finger-ends dug his shoulder warningly. They moved along somewhat more naturally, so far as Fafhrd's tied-up leg allowed.

"Gods, what an easy life the Guild-beggars have," the other niche-guard observed to his mate. "What slack discipline and low standards of skill! Perfect, my sacred butt! You'd think a child could see through those disguises."

"Doubtless some children do," his mate retorted. "But their dear mothers and fathers only drop a tear and a coin or give a kick. Grown folk go blind, lost in their toil and dreams, unless they have a profession such as thieving which keeps them mindful of things as they really are."

Resisting the impulse to ponder this sage

philosophy, and glad they would not have to undergo a Beggarmaster's shrewd inspection—truly, thought Fafhrd, Kos of the Dooms seemed to be leading him direct to Krovas and perhaps head-chopping *would* be the order of the night—he and the Mouser went watchfully and slowly on. And now they began to hear voices, mostly curt and clipped ones, and other noises.

They passed some doorways they'd liked to have paused at, to study the activities inside, yet the most they dared do was slow down a bit more. Fortunately most of the doorways were wide, permitting a fairly long view.

Very interesting were some of those activities. In one room young boys were being trained to pick pouches and slit purses. They'd approach from behind an instructor, and if he heard scuff of bare foot or felt touch of dipping hand—or, worst, heard *clunk* of dropped leaden mock-coin—that boy would

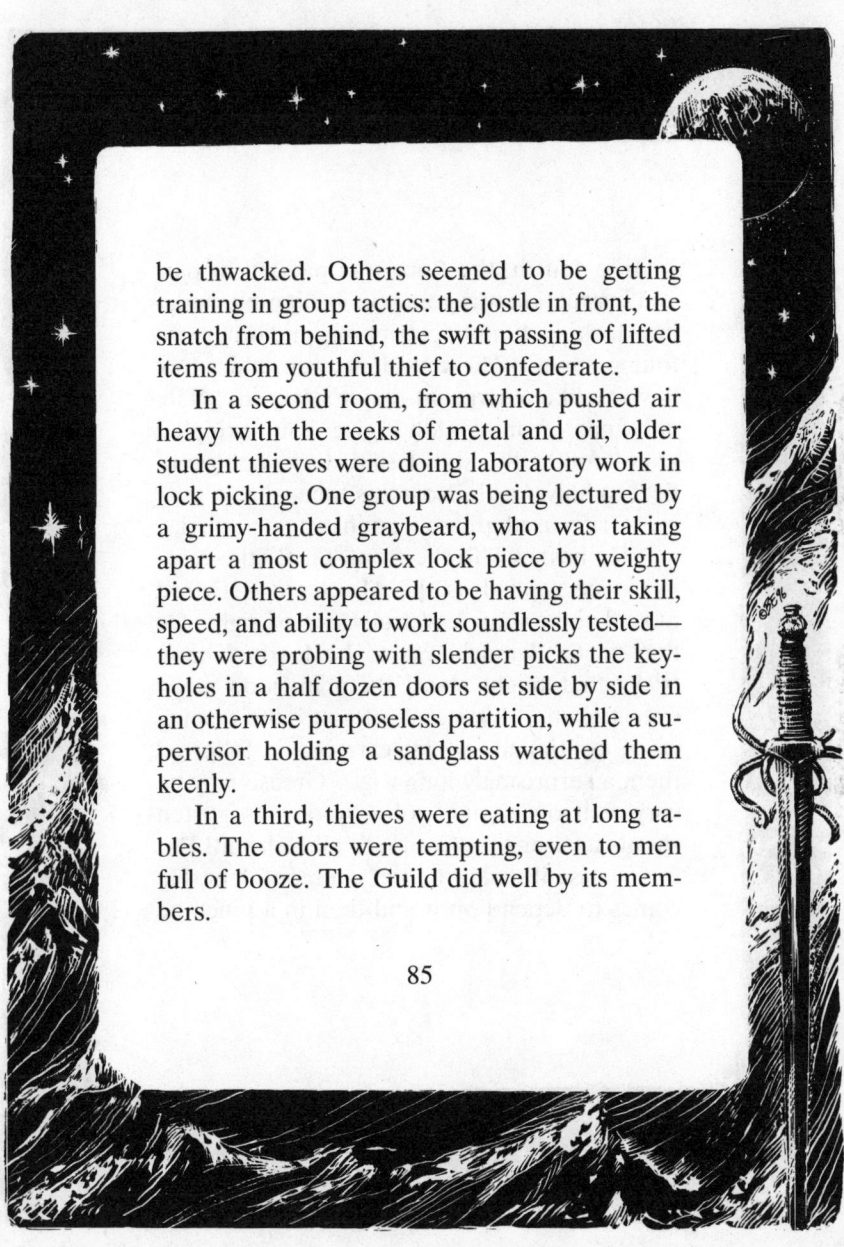

be thwacked. Others seemed to be getting training in group tactics: the jostle in front, the snatch from behind, the swift passing of lifted items from youthful thief to confederate.

In a second room, from which pushed air heavy with the reeks of metal and oil, older student thieves were doing laboratory work in lock picking. One group was being lectured by a grimy-handed graybeard, who was taking apart a most complex lock piece by weighty piece. Others appeared to be having their skill, speed, and ability to work soundlessly tested—they were probing with slender picks the keyholes in a half dozen doors set side by side in an otherwise purposeless partition, while a supervisor holding a sandglass watched them keenly.

In a third, thieves were eating at long tables. The odors were tempting, even to men full of booze. The Guild did well by its members.

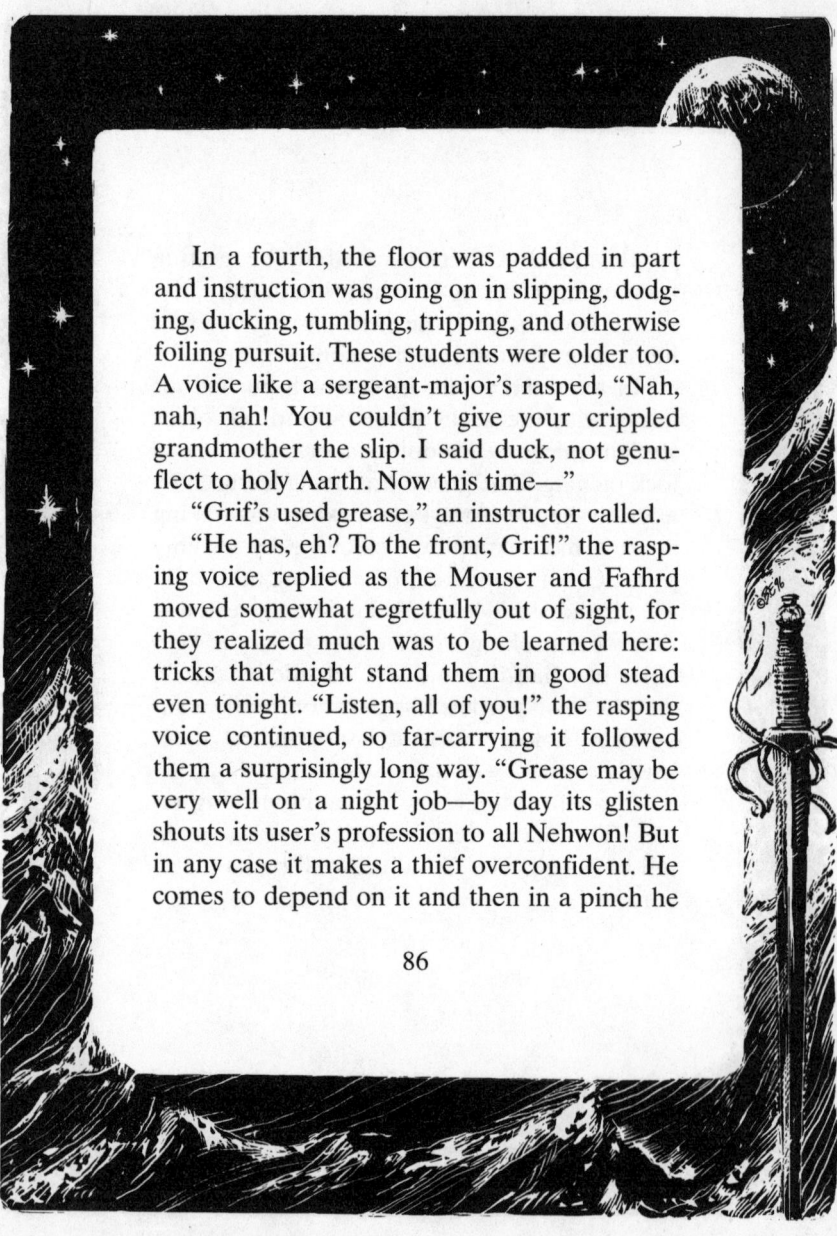

In a fourth, the floor was padded in part and instruction was going on in slipping, dodging, ducking, tumbling, tripping, and otherwise foiling pursuit. These students were older too. A voice like a sergeant-major's rasped, "Nah, nah, nah! You couldn't give your crippled grandmother the slip. I said duck, not genuflect to holy Aarth. Now this time—"

"Grif's used grease," an instructor called.

"He has, eh? To the front, Grif!" the rasping voice replied as the Mouser and Fafhrd moved somewhat regretfully out of sight, for they realized much was to be learned here: tricks that might stand them in good stead even tonight. "Listen, all of you!" the rasping voice continued, so far-carrying it followed them a surprisingly long way. "Grease may be very well on a night job—by day its glisten shouts its user's profession to all Nehwon! But in any case it makes a thief overconfident. He comes to depend on it and then in a pinch he finds he's forgot to apply it. Also its aroma can betray him. Here we work always dry-skinned—save for natural sweat!—as all of you were told first night. Bend over, Grif. Grasp your ankles. Straighten your knees."

More thwacks, followed by yelps of pain, distant now, since the Mouser and Fafhrd were halfway up the end-stairs, Fafhrd vaulting somewhat laboriously as he grasped curving banister and swaddled sword.

The second floor duplicated the first, but was as luxurious as the other had been bare. Down the long corridor lamps and filigreed incense pots pendant from the ceiling alternated, diffusing a mild light and spicy smell. The walls were richly draped, the floor thick-carpeted. Yet this corridor was empty too and, moreover, *completely* silent. After a glance at each other, they started off boldly. The first door, wide open, showed an untenanted room full of racks of garments, rich and plain, spotless and filthy,

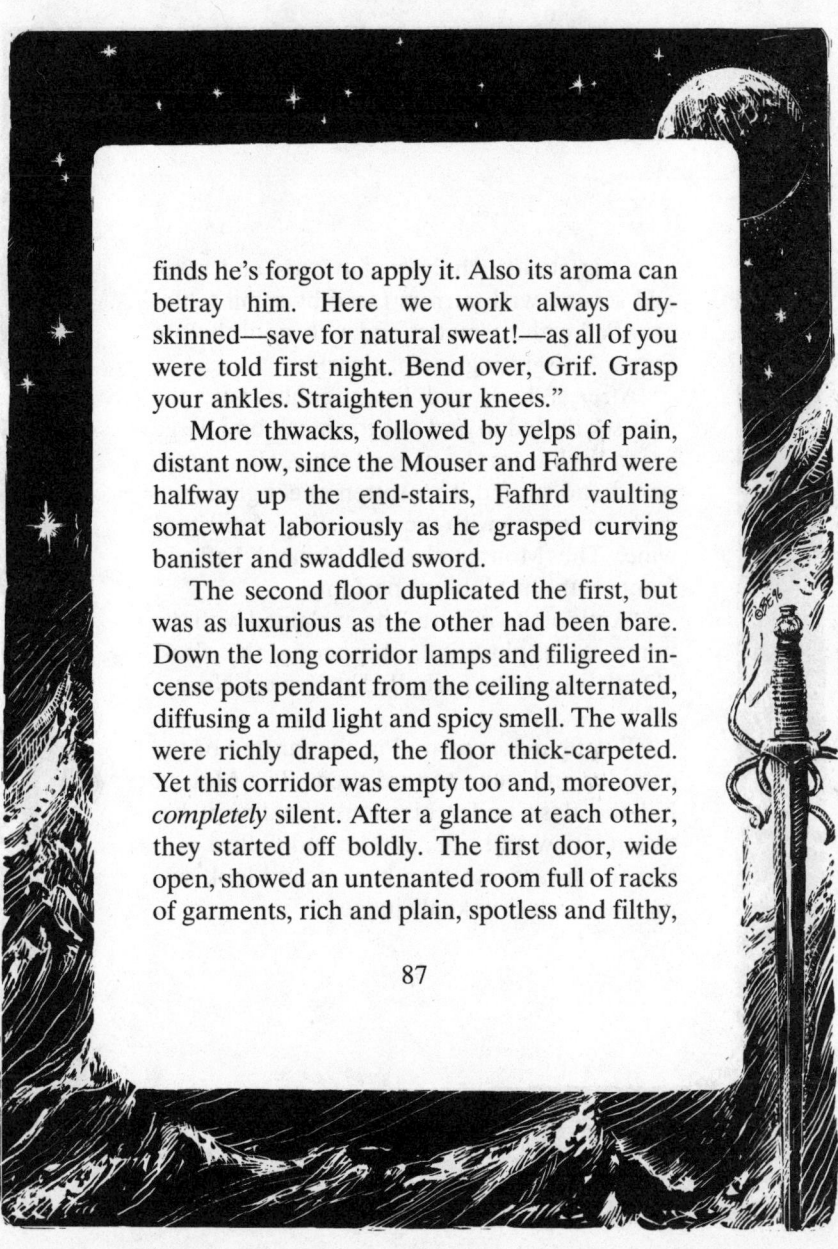

also wig stands, shelves of beards and such, and several wall mirrors faced by small tables crowded with cosmetics and with stools before them. A disguising room, clearly.

After a look and listen either way, the Mouser darted in and out to snatch up a large green flask from the nearest table. He unstoppered and sniffed it. A rotten-sweet gardenia-reek contended with the nose-sting of spirits of wine. The Mouser sloshed his and Fafhrd's fronts with this dubious perfume.

"Antidote to ordure," he explained with the pomp of a physician, stoppering the flask. "Don't want to be parboiled by Krovas. No, no, no."

Two figures appeared at the far end of the corridor and came toward them. The Mouser hid the flask under his cloak, holding it between elbow and side, and he and Fafhrd continued onward—to turn back would look suspicious, both drunkenly judged.

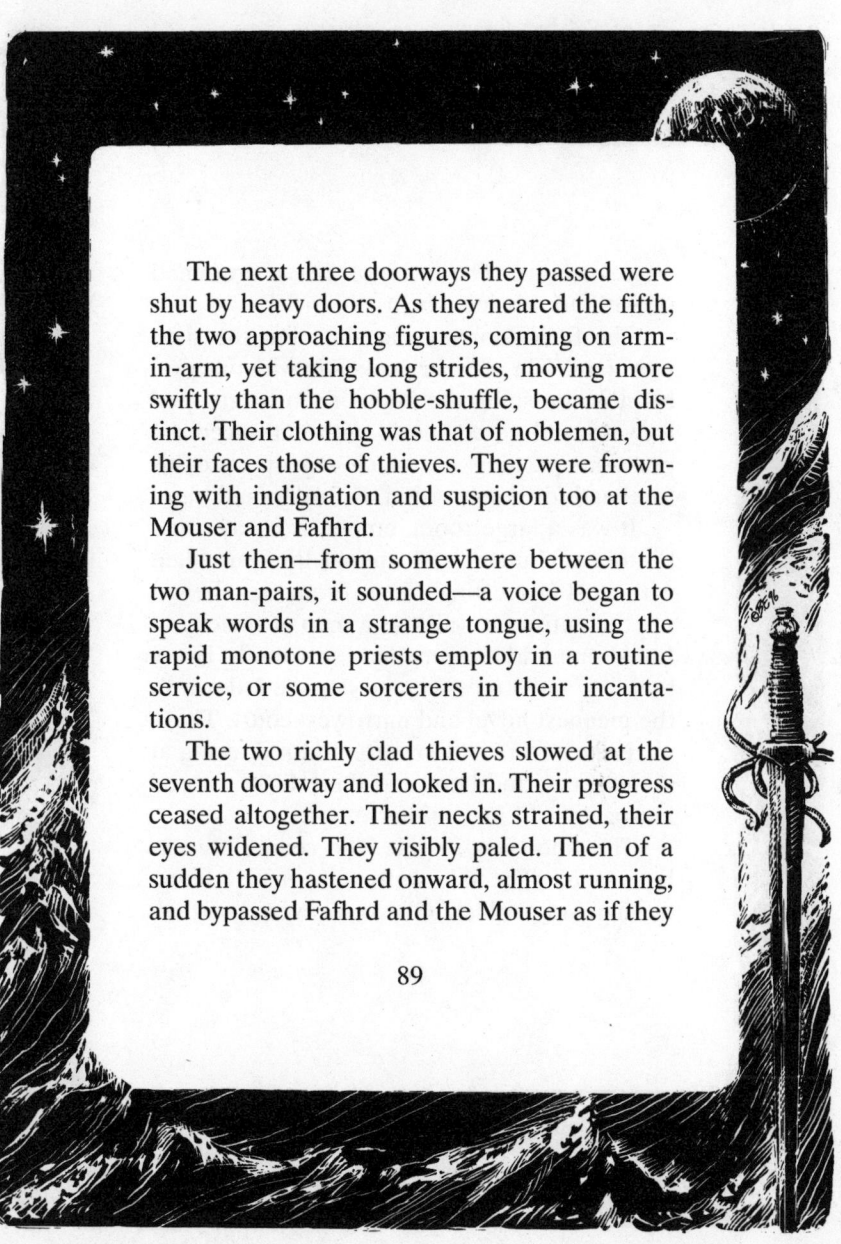

The next three doorways they passed were shut by heavy doors. As they neared the fifth, the two approaching figures, coming on arm-in-arm, yet taking long strides, moving more swiftly than the hobble-shuffle, became distinct. Their clothing was that of noblemen, but their faces those of thieves. They were frowning with indignation and suspicion too at the Mouser and Fafhrd.

Just then—from somewhere between the two man-pairs, it sounded—a voice began to speak words in a strange tongue, using the rapid monotone priests employ in a routine service, or some sorcerers in their incantations.

The two richly clad thieves slowed at the seventh doorway and looked in. Their progress ceased altogether. Their necks strained, their eyes widened. They visibly paled. Then of a sudden they hastened onward, almost running, and bypassed Fafhrd and the Mouser as if they

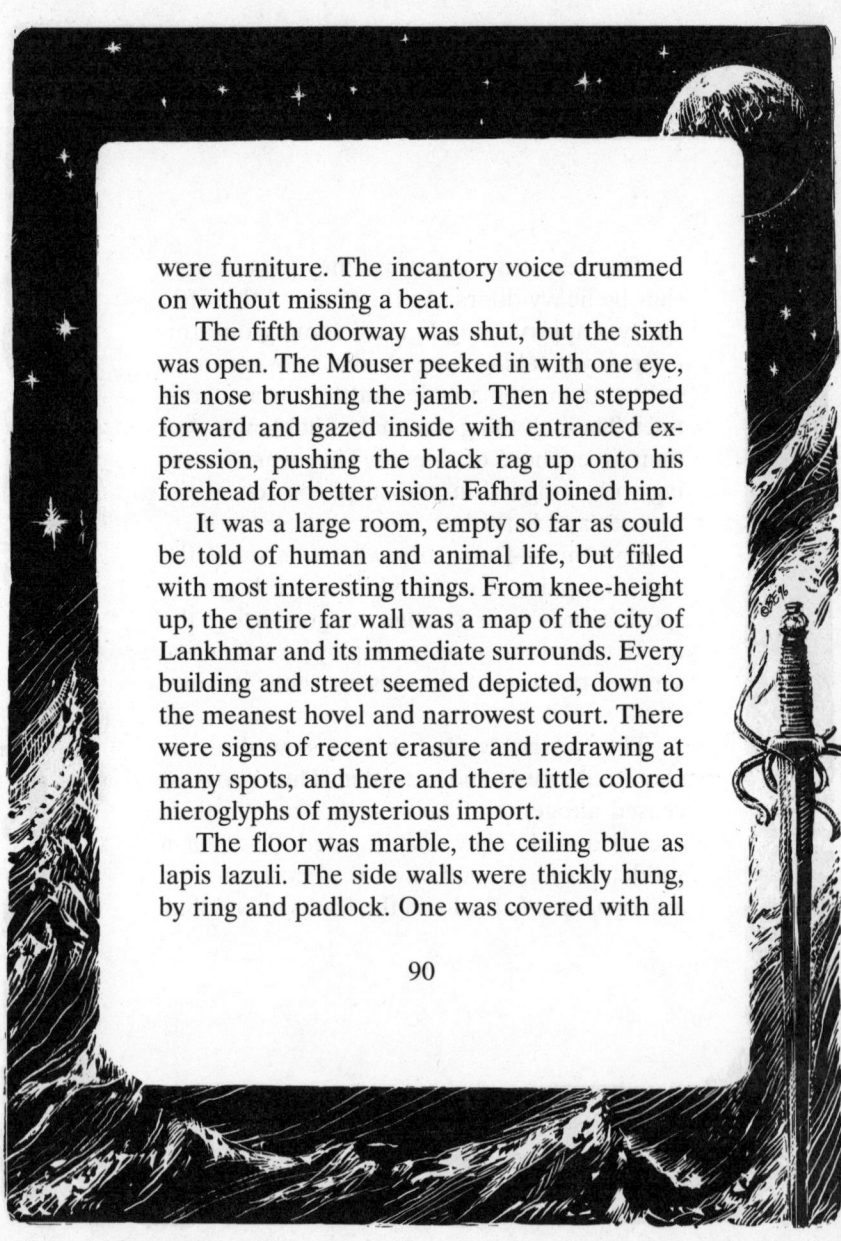

were furniture. The incantory voice drummed on without missing a beat.

The fifth doorway was shut, but the sixth was open. The Mouser peeked in with one eye, his nose brushing the jamb. Then he stepped forward and gazed inside with entranced expression, pushing the black rag up onto his forehead for better vision. Fafhrd joined him.

It was a large room, empty so far as could be told of human and animal life, but filled with most interesting things. From knee-height up, the entire far wall was a map of the city of Lankhmar and its immediate surrounds. Every building and street seemed depicted, down to the meanest hovel and narrowest court. There were signs of recent erasure and redrawing at many spots, and here and there little colored hieroglyphs of mysterious import.

The floor was marble, the ceiling blue as lapis lazuli. The side walls were thickly hung, by ring and padlock. One was covered with all

manner of thieves' tools, from a huge thick pry-bar that looked as if it could unseat the universe, or at least the door of the Overlord's treasure-vault, to a rod so slim it might be an elf-queen's wand and seemingly designed to telescope out and fish from distance for precious gauds on milady's spindle-legged, ivory-topped vanity table; the other wall had on it all sorts of quaint, gold-gleaming and jewel-flashing objects, evidently mementos chosen for their oddity from the spoils of memorable burglaries, from a female mask of thin gold, breathlessly beautiful in its features and contours, but thickly set with rubies simulating the spots of the pox in its fever-stage, to a knife whose blade was wedge-shaped diamonds set side by side and this diamond cutting-edge looking razor-sharp.

All about were tables set chiefly with models of dwelling houses and other buildings, accurate to the last minutia, it looked, of ventilation hole under roof gutter and ground-level drain hole, of creviced wall and smooth. Many were cut away in partial or entire section to show the layout of rooms, closets, strongrooms, doorways, corridors, secret passages, smoke-ways, and air-ways in equal detail.

In the center of the room was a bare roundtable of ebony and ivory squares. About it were set seven straight-backed but well-padded chairs, the one facing the map and away from the Mouser and Fafhrd being higher backed and wider armed than the others—a chief's chair, likely that of Krovas.

The Mouser tiptoed forward, irresistibly drawn, but Fafhrd's left hand clamped down on his shoulder like the iron mitten of a Mingol cataphract and drew him irresistibly back.

Scowling his disapproval, the Northerner brushed down the black rag over the Mouser's eyes again, and with his crutch-hand thumbed ahead; then set off in that direction in most

carefully calculated, silent hops. With a shrug of disappointment the Mouser followed.

As soon as they had turned away from the doorway, but before they were out of sight, a neatly black-bearded, crop-haired head came like a serpent's around the side of the highest-backed chair and gazed after them from deep-sunken yet glinting eyes. Next a snake-supple, long hand followed the head out, crossed thin lips with ophidian forefinger for silence, and then finger-beckoned the two pairs of dark-tunicked men who were standing to either side of the doorway, their backs to the corridor wall, each of the four gripping a curvy knife in one hand and a dark leather, lead-weighted bludgeon in the other.

When Fafhrd was halfway to the seventh doorway, from which the monotonous yet sinister recitation continued to well, there shot out through it a slender, whey-faced youth, his narrow hands clapped over his mouth, under

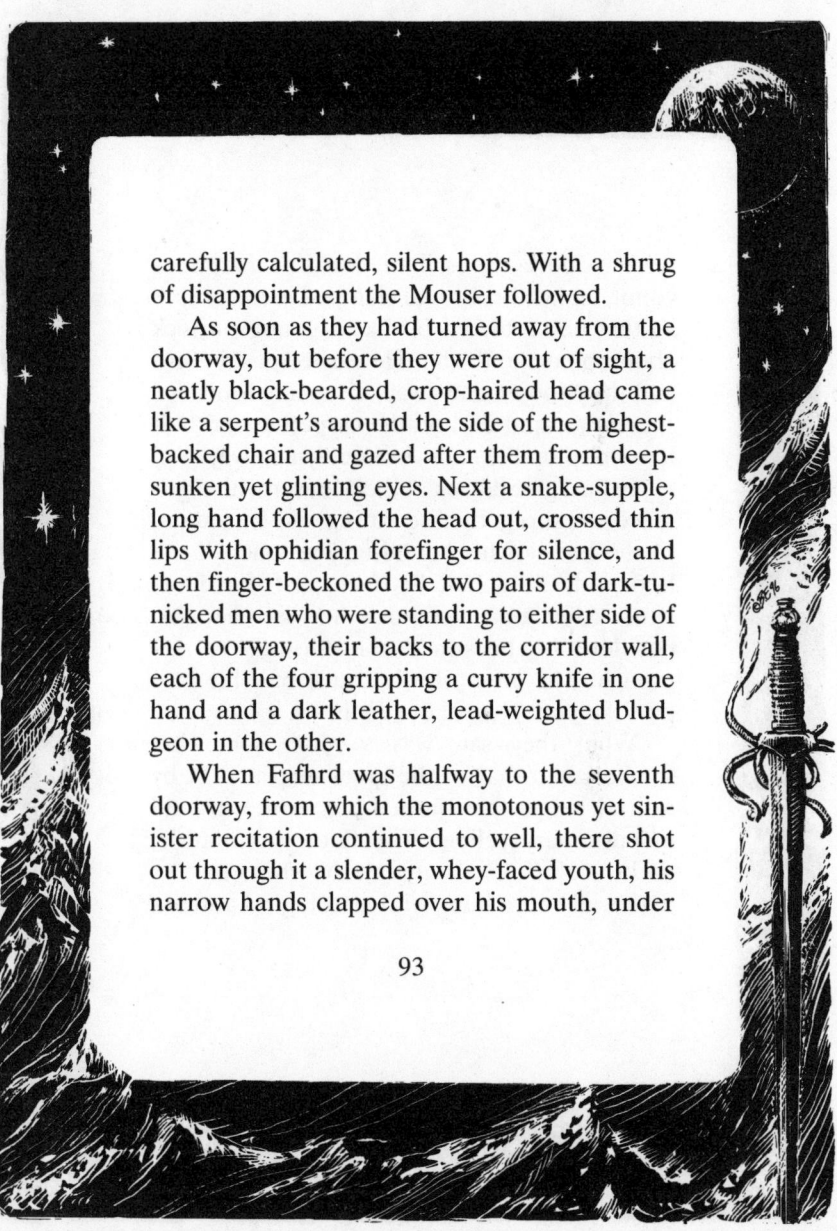

terror-wide eyes, as if to shut in screams or vomit, and with a broom clamped in an armpit, so that he seemed a bit like a young warlock about to take to the air. He dashed past Fafhrd and the Mouser and away, his racing footsteps sounding rapid-dull on the carpeting and hollow-sharp on the stairs before dying away.

Fafhrd gazed back at the Mouser with a grimace and shrug, then squatting one-legged until the knee of his bound-up leg touched the floor, advanced half his face past the doorjamb. After a bit, without otherwise changing position, he beckoned the Mouser to approach. The latter slowly thrust half his face past the jamb, just above Fafhrd's.

What they saw was a room somewhat smaller than that of the great map and lit by central lamps that burned blue-white instead of customary yellow. The floor was marble, darkly colorful and complexly whorled. The dark walls were hung with astrological and anthropomantic charts and instruments of magic and shelved with cryptically labeled porcelain jars and also with vitreous flasks and glass pipes of the oddest shapes, some filled with colored fluids, but many gleamingly empty. At the foot of the walls, where the shadows were thickest, broken and discarded stuff was irregularly heaped, as if swept out of the way and forgot, and here and there opened a large rathole.

In the center of the room and brightly illuminated by contrast was a long table with thick top and many stout legs. The Mouser thought fleetingly of a centipede and then of the bar at the Eel, for the tabletop was densely stained and scarred by many a spilled elixir and many a deep black burn by fire or acid or both.

In the midst of the table an alembic was working. The lamp's flame—deep blue, this one—kept a-boil in the large crystal cucurbit a dark, viscid fluid with here and there diamond glints. From out of the thick, seething stuff, strands of a darker vapor streamed upward to crowd through the cucurbit's narrow mouth and stain—oddly, with bright scarlet—the transparent head and then, dead black now, flow down the narrow pipe from the head into a spherical crystal receiver, larger even than the cucurbit, and there curl and weave about like so many coils of living black cord—an endless, skinny, ebon serpent.

Behind the left end of the table stood a tall, yet hunchbacked man in black robe and hood which shadowed more than hid a face of which the most prominent features were a long, thick, pointed nose with out-jutting, almost chinless mouth just below. His complexion was sallow-gray like clay and a short-haired bristly, gray beard grew high on his wide cheeks. From under a receding forehead and bushy gray brows, wide-set eyes looked intently down at an age-browned scroll, which his disgustingly

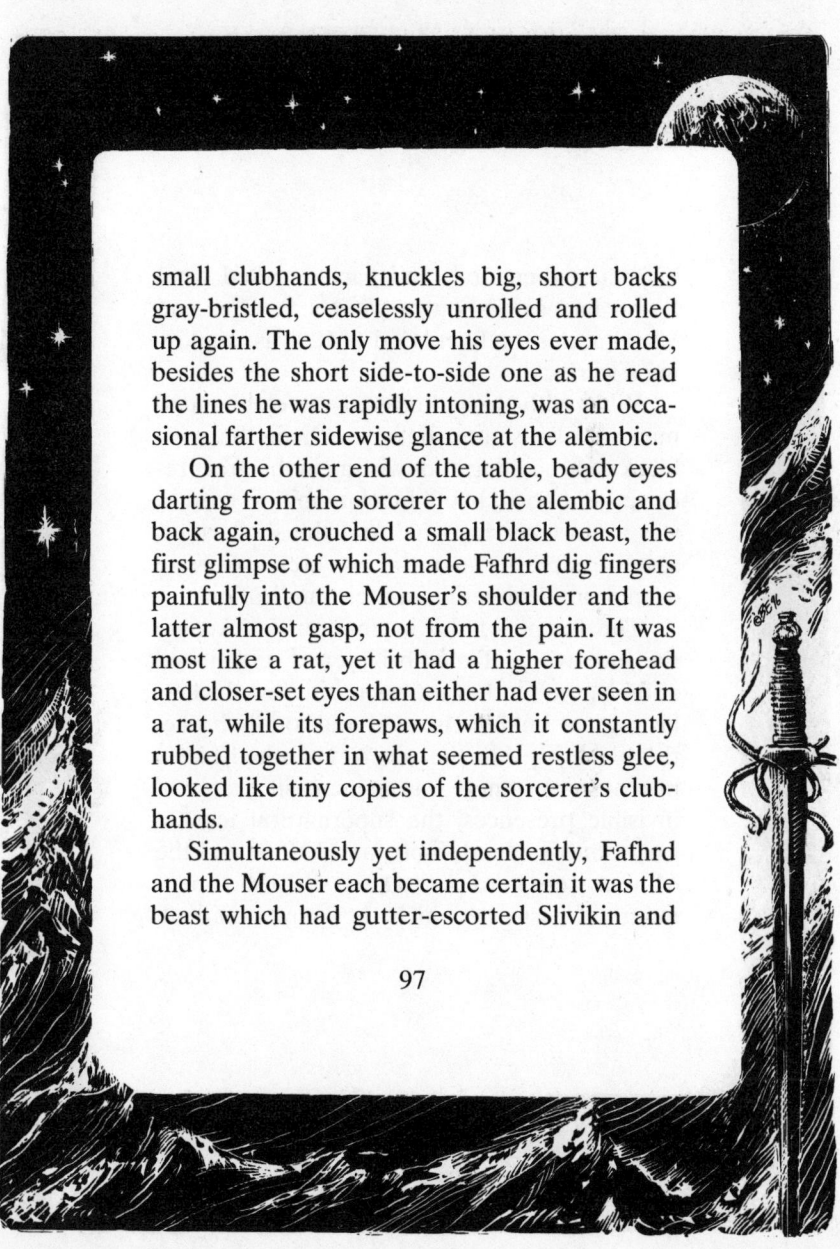

small clubhands, knuckles big, short backs gray-bristled, ceaselessly unrolled and rolled up again. The only move his eyes ever made, besides the short side-to-side one as he read the lines he was rapidly intoning, was an occasional farther sidewise glance at the alembic.

On the other end of the table, beady eyes darting from the sorcerer to the alembic and back again, crouched a small black beast, the first glimpse of which made Fafhrd dig fingers painfully into the Mouser's shoulder and the latter almost gasp, not from the pain. It was most like a rat, yet it had a higher forehead and closer-set eyes than either had ever seen in a rat, while its forepaws, which it constantly rubbed together in what seemed restless glee, looked like tiny copies of the sorcerer's clubhands.

Simultaneously yet independently, Fafhrd and the Mouser each became certain it was the beast which had gutter-escorted Slivikin and

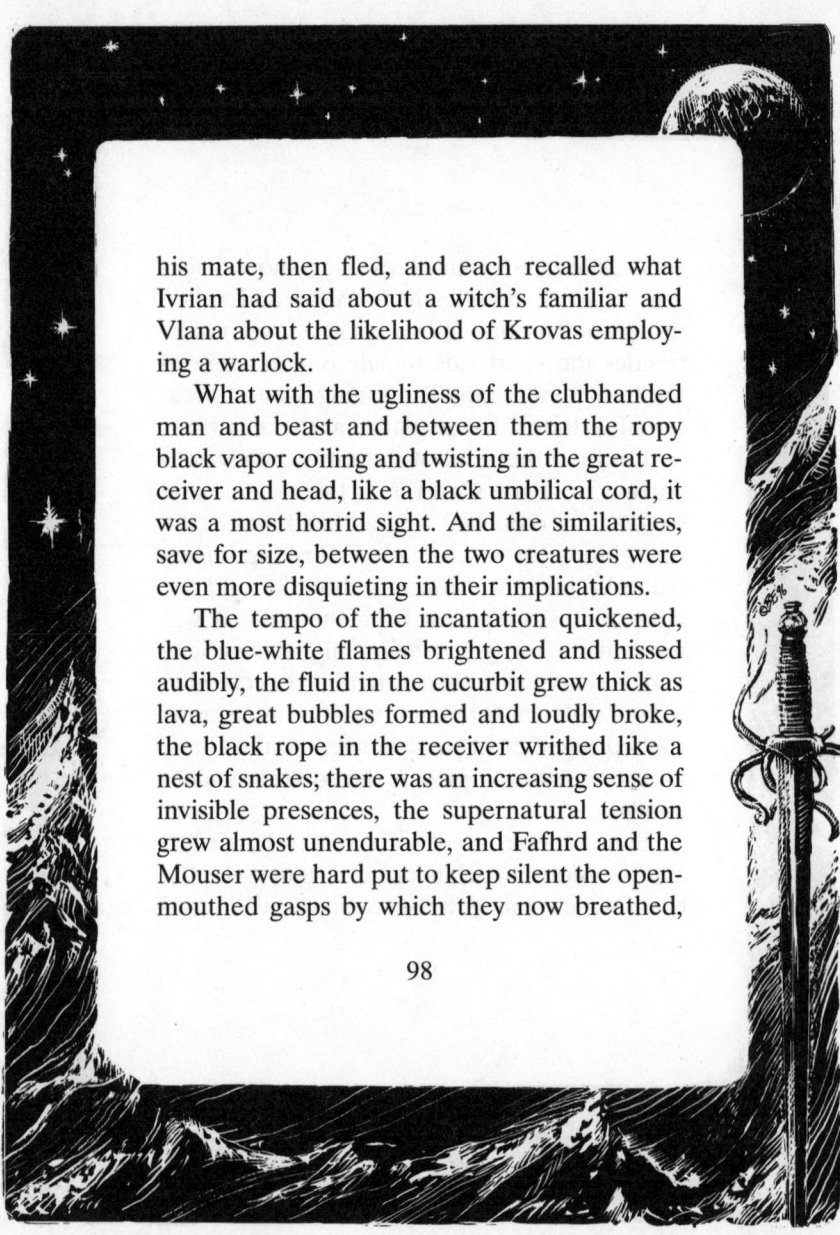

his mate, then fled, and each recalled what Ivrian had said about a witch's familiar and Vlana about the likelihood of Krovas employing a warlock.

What with the ugliness of the clubhanded man and beast and between them the ropy black vapor coiling and twisting in the great receiver and head, like a black umbilical cord, it was a most horrid sight. And the similarities, save for size, between the two creatures were even more disquieting in their implications.

The tempo of the incantation quickened, the blue-white flames brightened and hissed audibly, the fluid in the cucurbit grew thick as lava, great bubbles formed and loudly broke, the black rope in the receiver writhed like a nest of snakes; there was an increasing sense of invisible presences, the supernatural tension grew almost unendurable, and Fafhrd and the Mouser were hard put to keep silent the open-mouthed gasps by which they now breathed, and each feared his heartbeat could be heard cubits away.

Abruptly the incantation peaked and broke off, like a drum struck very hard, then instantly silenced by palm and fingers outspread against the head. With a bright flash and dull explosion, cracks innumerable appeared in the cucurbit; its crystal became white and opaque, yet it did not shatter or drip. The head lifted a span, hung there, fell back. While two black nooses appeared among the coils in the receiver and suddenly narrowed until they were only two big black knots.

The sorcerer grinned, rolling up the end of the parchment with a snap, and shifted his gaze from the receiver to his familiar, while the latter chittered shrilly and bounded up and down in rapture.

"Silence, Slivikin! Comes now your time to race and strain and sweat," the sorcerer cried, speaking pidgin Lankhmarese now, but so rapidly and in so squeakingly high-pitched a voice that Fafhrd and the Mouser could barely follow him. They did, however, both realize they had been completely mistaken as to the identity of Slivikin. In moment of disaster, the fat thief had called to the witch-beast for help rather than to his human comrade.

"Yes, master," Slivikin squeaked back no less clearly, in an instant revising the Mouser's opinions about talking animals. He continued in the same fifelike, fawning tones, "Harkening in obedience, Hristomilo."

Now they knew the sorcerer's name too.

Hristomilo ordered in whiplash pipings, "To your appointed work! See to it you summon an ample sufficiency of feasters! I want the bodies stripped to skeletons, so the bruises of the enchanted smog and all evidence of death by suffocation will be vanished utterly. But forget not the loot! On your mission, now —depart!"

Slivikin, who at every command had bobbed his head in manner reminiscent of his bouncing, now squealed, "I'll see it done!" and gray-lightninglike leaped a long leap to the floor and down an inky rathole.

Hristomilo, rubbing together his disgusting clubhands much as Slivikin had his, cried chucklingly, "What Slevyas lost, my magic has rewon!"

Fafhrd and the Mouser drew back out of the doorway, partly with the thought that since neither his incantation and his alembic, nor his familiar now required his unblinking attention, Hristomilo would surely look up and spot them; partly in revulsion from what they had seen and heard; and in poignant if useless pity for Slevyas, whoever he might be, and for the other unknown victims of the ratlike and conceivably rat-related sorcerer's death spells, poor strangers already dead and due to have their flesh eaten from their bones.

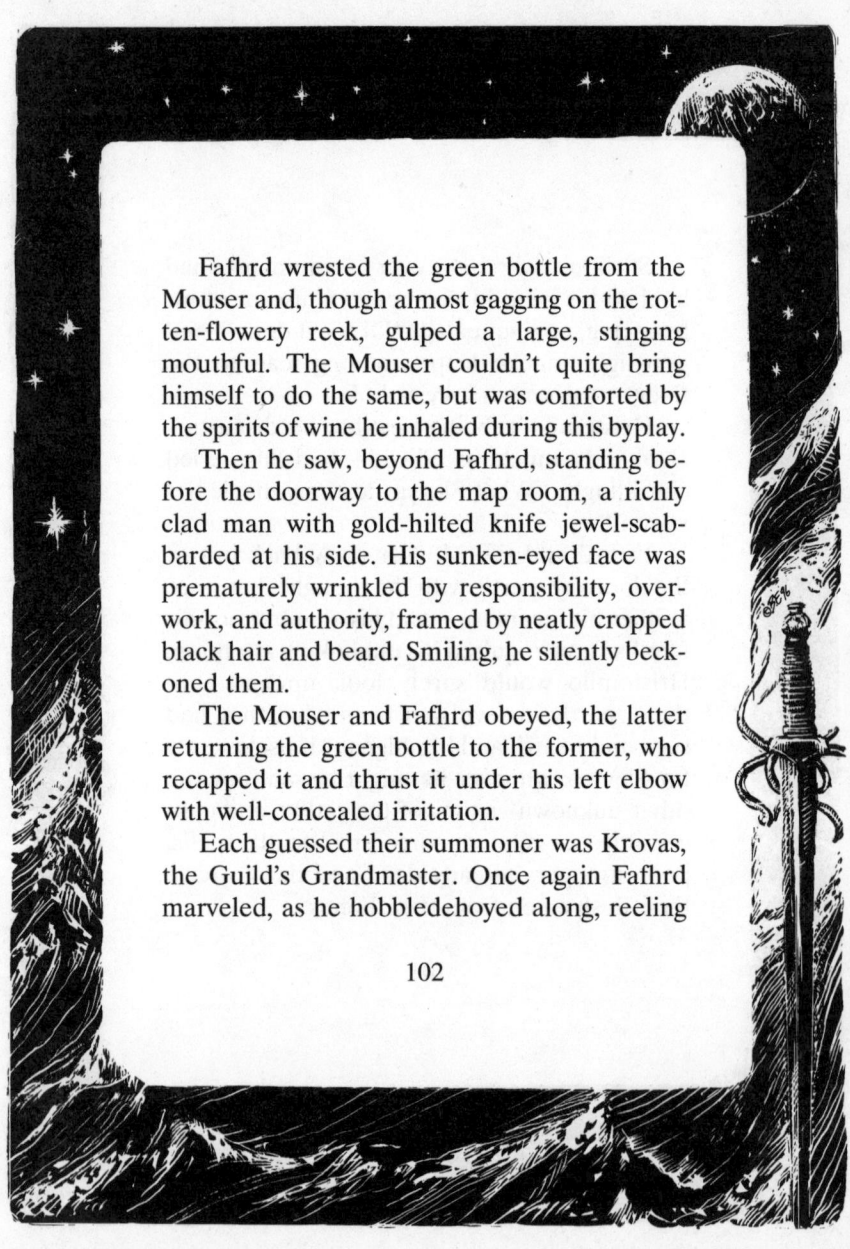

Fafhrd wrested the green bottle from the Mouser and, though almost gagging on the rotten-flowery reek, gulped a large, stinging mouthful. The Mouser couldn't quite bring himself to do the same, but was comforted by the spirits of wine he inhaled during this byplay.

Then he saw, beyond Fafhrd, standing before the doorway to the map room, a richly clad man with gold-hilted knife jewel-scabbarded at his side. His sunken-eyed face was prematurely wrinkled by responsibility, overwork, and authority, framed by neatly cropped black hair and beard. Smiling, he silently beckoned them.

The Mouser and Fafhrd obeyed, the latter returning the green bottle to the former, who recapped it and thrust it under his left elbow with well-concealed irritation.

Each guessed their summoner was Krovas, the Guild's Grandmaster. Once again Fafhrd marveled, as he hobbledehoyed along, reeling and belching, how Kos or the Fates were guiding him to his target tonight. The Mouser, more alert and more apprehensive too, was reminding himself that they had been directed by the niche-guards to report to Krovas, so that the situation, if not developing quite in accord with his own misty plans, was still not deviating disastrously.

Yet not even his alertness, nor Fafhrd's primeval instincts, gave him forewarning as they followed Krovas into the map room.

Two steps inside, each of them was shoulder-grabbed and bludgeon-menaced by a pair of ruffians further armed with knives tucked in their belts.

They judged it wise to make no resistance, on this one occasion at least bearing out the Mouser's mouthings about the supreme caution of drunken men.

"All secure, Grandmaster," one of the ruffians rapped out.

Krovas swung the highest-backed chair around and sat down, eyeing them coolly yet searchingly.

"What brings two stinking, drunken beggar-Guildsmen into the top-restricted precincts of the masters?" he asked quietly.

The Mouser felt the sweat of relief bead his forehead. The disguises he had brilliantly conceived were still working, taking in even the head man, though he had spotted Fafhrd's tipsiness. Resuming his blind-man manner, he quavered, "We were directed by the guard above the Cheap Street door to report to you in person, great Krovas, the Night Beggarmaster being on furlough for reasons of sexual hygiene. Tonight we've made good haul!" And fumbling in his purse, ignoring as far as possible the tightened grip on his shoulders, he brought out the golden coin given him by the sentimental courtesan and displayed it tremble-handed.

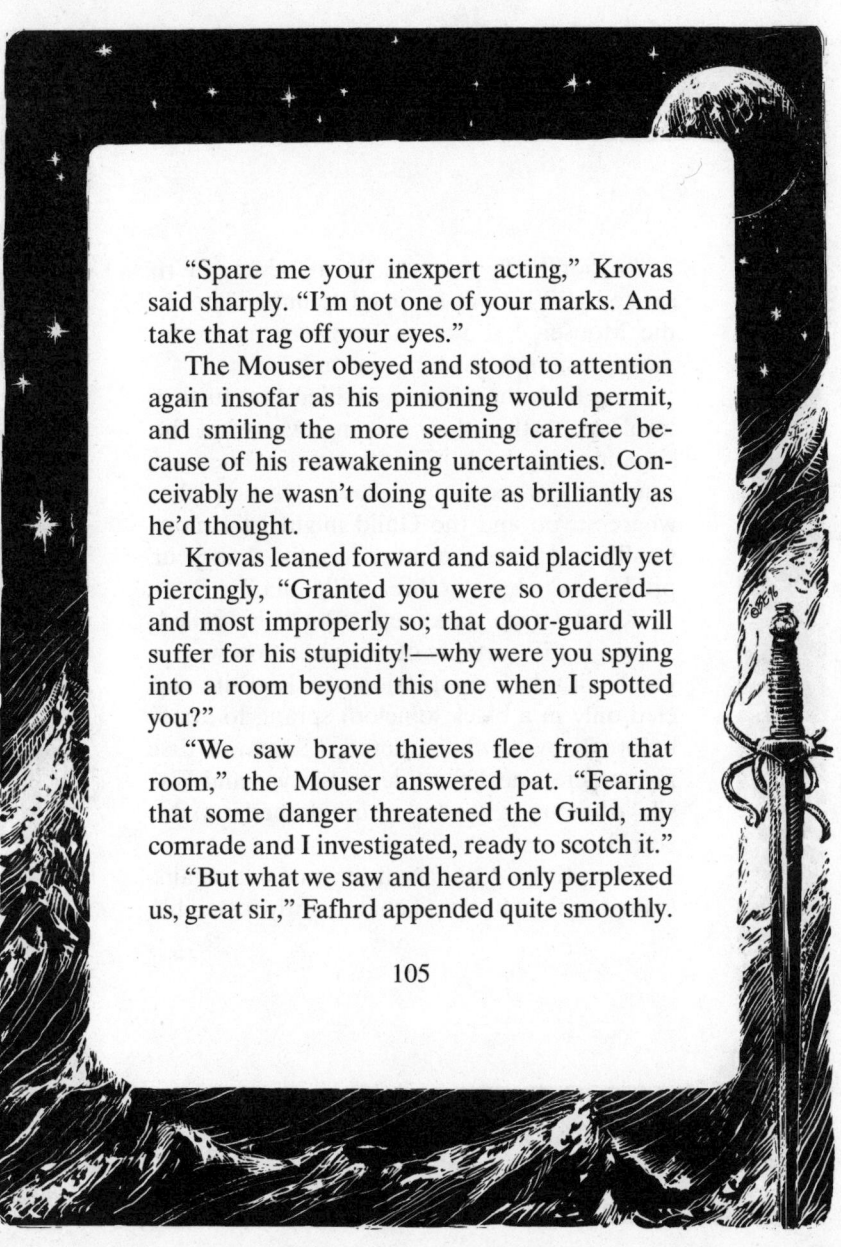

"Spare me your inexpert acting," Krovas said sharply. "I'm not one of your marks. And take that rag off your eyes."

The Mouser obeyed and stood to attention again insofar as his pinioning would permit, and smiling the more seeming carefree because of his reawakening uncertainties. Conceivably he wasn't doing quite as brilliantly as he'd thought.

Krovas leaned forward and said placidly yet piercingly, "Granted you were so ordered—and most improperly so; that door-guard will suffer for his stupidity!—why were you spying into a room beyond this one when I spotted you?"

"We saw brave thieves flee from that room," the Mouser answered pat. "Fearing that some danger threatened the Guild, my comrade and I investigated, ready to scotch it."

"But what we saw and heard only perplexed us, great sir," Fafhrd appended quite smoothly.

"I didn't ask you, sot. Speak when you're spoken to," Krovas snapped at him. Then, to the Mouser, "You're an overweening rogue, most presumptuous for your rank."

In a flash the Mouser decided that further insolence, rather than fawning, was what the situation required. "That I am, sir," he said smugly. "For example, I have a master plan whereby you and the Guild might gain more wealth and power in three months than your predecessors have in three millennia."

Krovas' face darkened. "Boy!" he called. Through the curtains of an inner doorway, a youth with dark complexion of a Kleshite and clad only in a black loincloth sprang to kneel before Krovas, who ordered, "Summon first my sorcerer, next the thieves Slevyas and Fissif," whereupon the dark youth dashed into the corridor.

Then Krovas, his face its normal pale again, leaned back in his great chair, lightly rested his

sinewy arms on its great padded ones, and smilingly directed at the Mouser, "Speak your piece. Reveal to us this master plan."

Forcing his mind *not* to work on the surprising news that Slevyas was not victim but thief and not sorcery-slain but alive and available—why did Krovas want him *now*?—the Mouser threw back his head and, shaping his lips in a faint sneer, began, "You may laugh merrily at me, Grandmaster, but I'll warrant that in less than a score of heartbeats you'll be straining sober-faced to hear my least word. Like lightning, wit can strike anywhere, and the best of you in Lankhmar have age-honored blind spots for things obvious to us of outland birth. My master plan is but this: let Thieves' Guild under your iron autocracy seize supreme power in Lankhmar City, then in Lankhmar Land, next over all Nehwon, after which who knows what realms undreamt will know your suzerainty!"

The Mouser had spoken true in one respect: Krovas was no longer smiling. He was leaning forward a little and his face was darkening again, but whether from interest or anger it was too soon to say.

The Mouser continued, "For centuries the Guild's had more than the force and intelligence needed to make a *coup d'etat* a nine-finger certainty; today there's not one hair's chance in a bushy head of failure. It is the proper state of things that thieves rule other men. All Nature cries out for it. No need slay old Karstak Ovartamortes, merely overmaster, control, and so rule through him. You've already fee'd informers in every noble or wealthy house. Your post's better than the King of Kings'. You've a mercenary striking force permanently mobilized, should you have need of it, in the Slayers' Brotherhood. We Guild-beggars are your foragers. O great Krovas, the multitudes know that thievery rules Nehwon, nay, the universe, nay, more, the highest gods' abode! And the multitudes accept this, they balk only at the hypocrisy of the present arrangement, at the pretense that things are otherwise. Oh, give them their decent desire, great Krovas! Make it all open, honest and aboveboard, with thieves ruling in name as well as fact."

The Mouser spoke with passion, for the moment believing all he said, even the contradictions. The four ruffians gaped at him with wonder and not a little awe. They slackened their holds on him and on Fafhrd too.

But leaning back in his great chair again and smiling thinly and ominously, Krovas said coolly, "In *our* Guild intoxication is no excuse for folly, rather grounds for the extremest penalty. But I'm well aware your organized beggars operate under a laxer discipline. So I'll deign to explain to you, you wee drunken dreamer, that we thieves know well that, be-

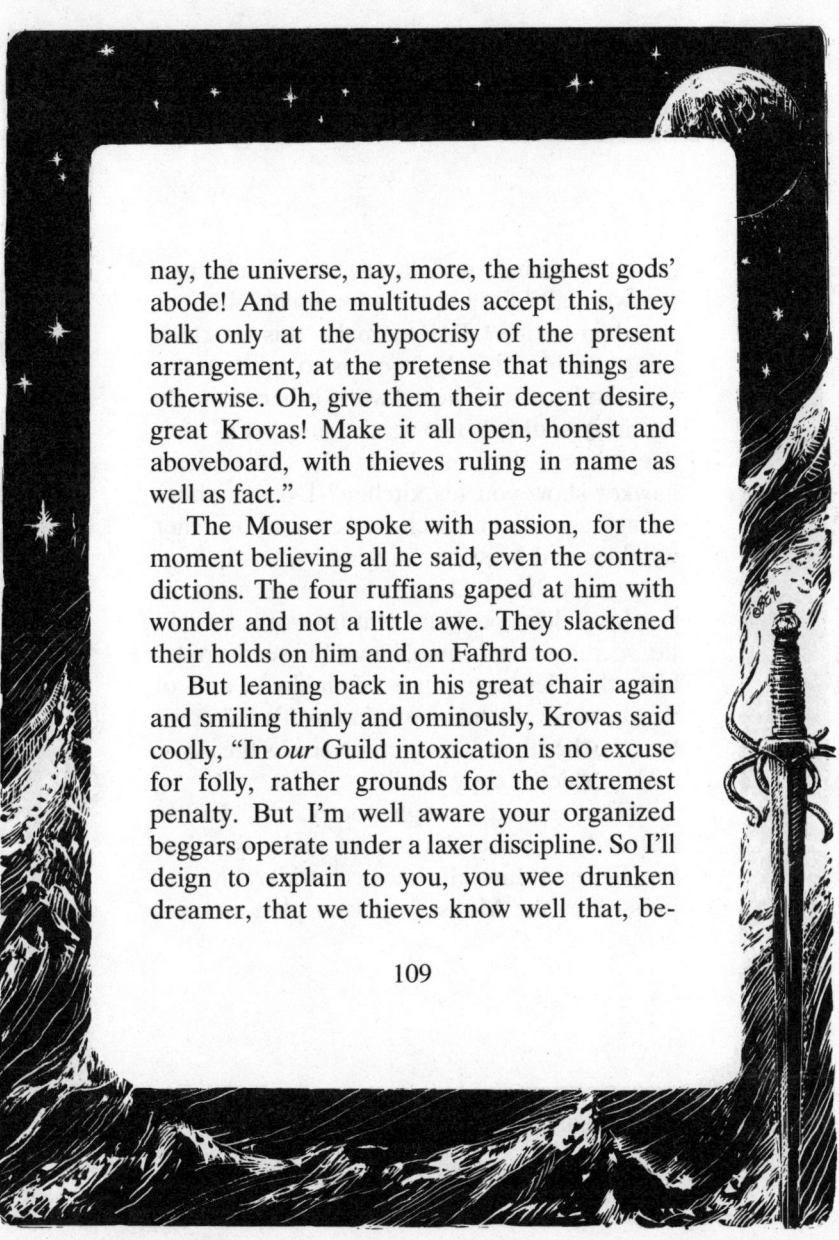

hind the scenes, we already rule Lankhmar, Nehwon, all life in sooth—for what is life but greed in action? But to make this an open thing would not only force us to take on ten thousand sorts of weary work others now do for us, it would also go against another of life's deep laws: illusion. Does the sweetmeats hawker show you his kitchen? Does a whore let average client watch her enamel-over her wrinkles and hoist her sagging breasts in cunning gauzy slings? Does a conjurer turn out for you his hidden pockets? Nature works by subtle, secret means—man's invisible seed, spider bite, the viewless spores of madness and of death, rocks that are born in earth's unknown bowels, the silent stars a-creep across the sky—and we thieves copy her."

"That's good enough poetry, sir," Fafhrd responded with undertone of angry derision, for he had himself been considerably impressed by the Mouser's master plan and was

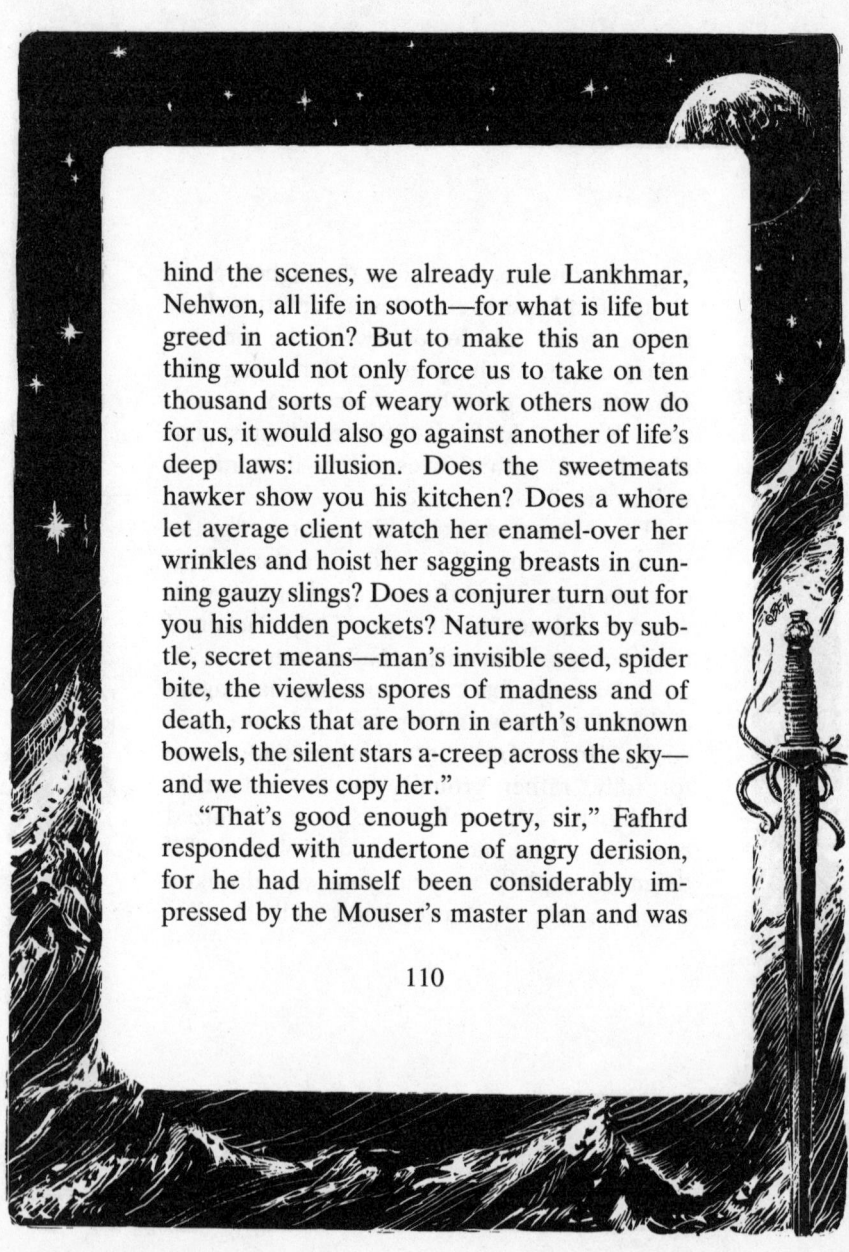

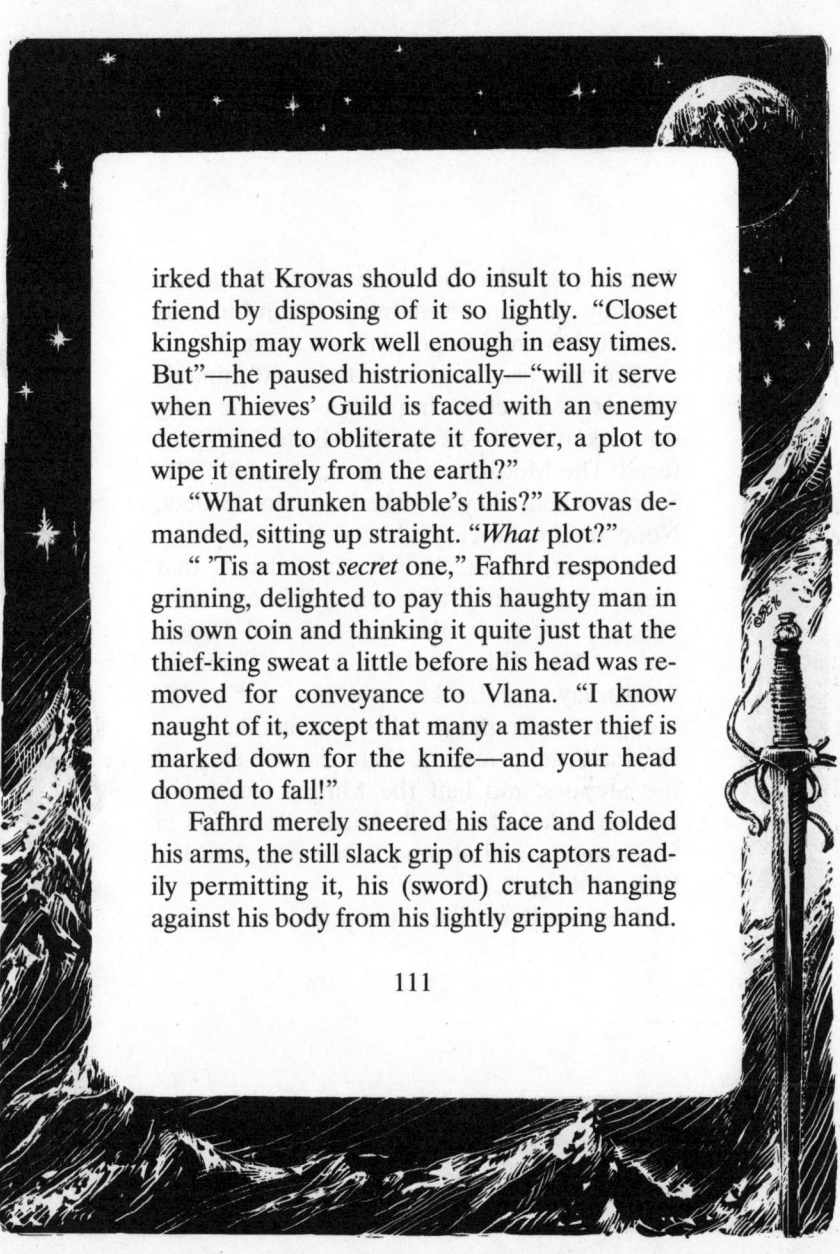

irked that Krovas should do insult to his new friend by disposing of it so lightly. "Closet kingship may work well enough in easy times. But"—he paused histrionically—"will it serve when Thieves' Guild is faced with an enemy determined to obliterate it forever, a plot to wipe it entirely from the earth?"

"What drunken babble's this?" Krovas demanded, sitting up straight. "*What* plot?"

" 'Tis a most *secret* one," Fafhrd responded grinning, delighted to pay this haughty man in his own coin and thinking it quite just that the thief-king sweat a little before his head was removed for conveyance to Vlana. "I know naught of it, except that many a master thief is marked down for the knife—and your head doomed to fall!"

Fafhrd merely sneered his face and folded his arms, the still slack grip of his captors readily permitting it, his (sword) crutch hanging against his body from his lightly gripping hand.

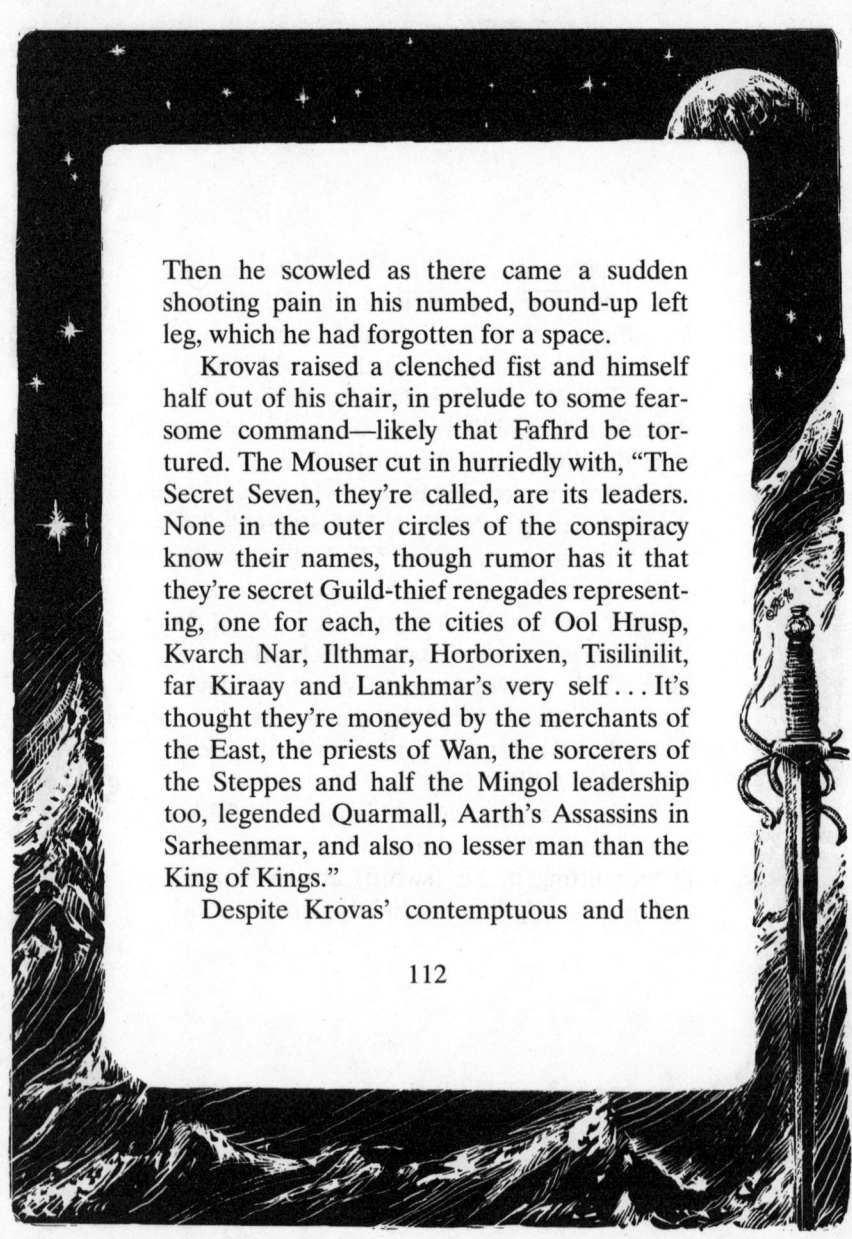

Then he scowled as there came a sudden shooting pain in his numbed, bound-up left leg, which he had forgotten for a space.

Krovas raised a clenched fist and himself half out of his chair, in prelude to some fearsome command—likely that Fafhrd be tortured. The Mouser cut in hurriedly with, "The Secret Seven, they're called, are its leaders. None in the outer circles of the conspiracy know their names, though rumor has it that they're secret Guild-thief renegades representing, one for each, the cities of Ool Hrusp, Kvarch Nar, Ilthmar, Horborixen, Tisilinilit, far Kiraay and Lankhmar's very self... It's thought they're moneyed by the merchants of the East, the priests of Wan, the sorcerers of the Steppes and half the Mingol leadership too, legended Quarmall, Aarth's Assassins in Sarheenmar, and also no lesser man than the King of Kings."

Despite Krovas' contemptuous and then

angry remarks, the ruffians holding the Mouser continued to harken to their captive with interest and respect, and they did not retighten their grip on him. His colorful revelations and melodramatic delivery held them, while Krovas' dry, cynical, philosophic observations largely went over their heads.

Hristomilo came gliding into the room then, his feet presumably taking swift, but very short steps, at any rate his black robe hung undisturbed to the marble floor despite his slithering speed.

There was a shock at his entrance. All eyes in the map room followed him, breaths were held, and the Mouser and Fafhrd felt the horny hands that gripped them shake just a little. Even Krovas' all-confident, world-weary expression became tense and guardedly uneasy. Clearly the sorcerer of the Thieves' Guild was more feared than loved by his chief employer and by the beneficiaries of his skills.

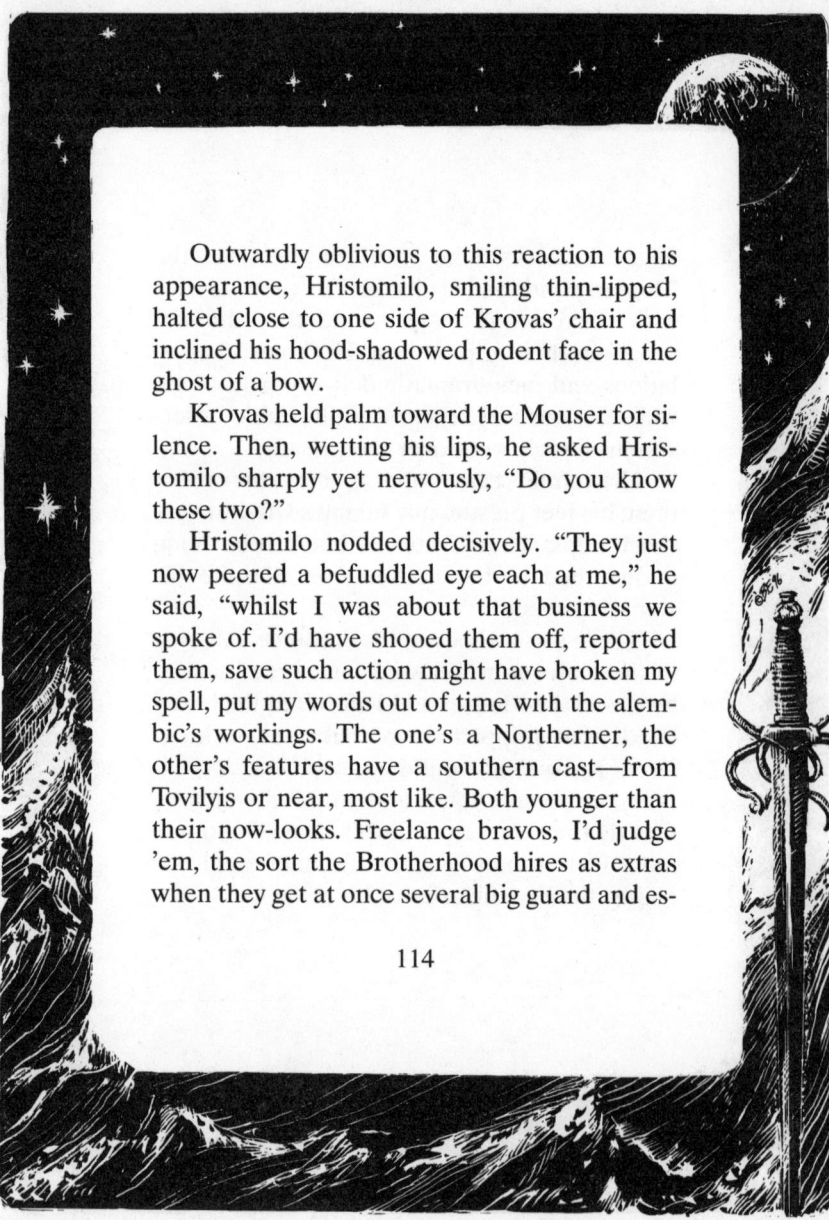

Outwardly oblivious to this reaction to his appearance, Hristomilo, smiling thin-lipped, halted close to one side of Krovas' chair and inclined his hood-shadowed rodent face in the ghost of a bow.

Krovas held palm toward the Mouser for silence. Then, wetting his lips, he asked Hristomilo sharply yet nervously, "Do you know these two?"

Hristomilo nodded decisively. "They just now peered a befuddled eye each at me," he said, "whilst I was about that business we spoke of. I'd have shooed them off, reported them, save such action might have broken my spell, put my words out of time with the alembic's workings. The one's a Northerner, the other's features have a southern cast—from Tovilyis or near, most like. Both younger than their now-looks. Freelance bravos, I'd judge 'em, the sort the Brotherhood hires as extras when they get at once several big guard and es-

cort jobs. Clumsily disguised now, of course, as beggars."

Fafhrd by yawning, the Mouser by pitying head shake tried to convey that all this was so much poor guesswork.

"That's all I can tell you without reading their minds," Hristomilo concluded. "Shall I fetch my lights and mirrors?"

"Not yet." Krovas turned face and shot a finger at the Mouser. "How do you know these things you rant about?—Secret Seven and all. Straight simplest answer now—no rodomontades."

The Mouser replied most glibly: "There's a new courtesan dwells on Pimp Street—Tyarya her name, tall, beauteous, but hunchbacked, which oddly delights many of her clients. Now Tyarya loves me 'cause my maimed eyes match her twisted spine, or from simple pity of my blindness—*she* believes it!—and youth, or from some odd itch, like her clients' for

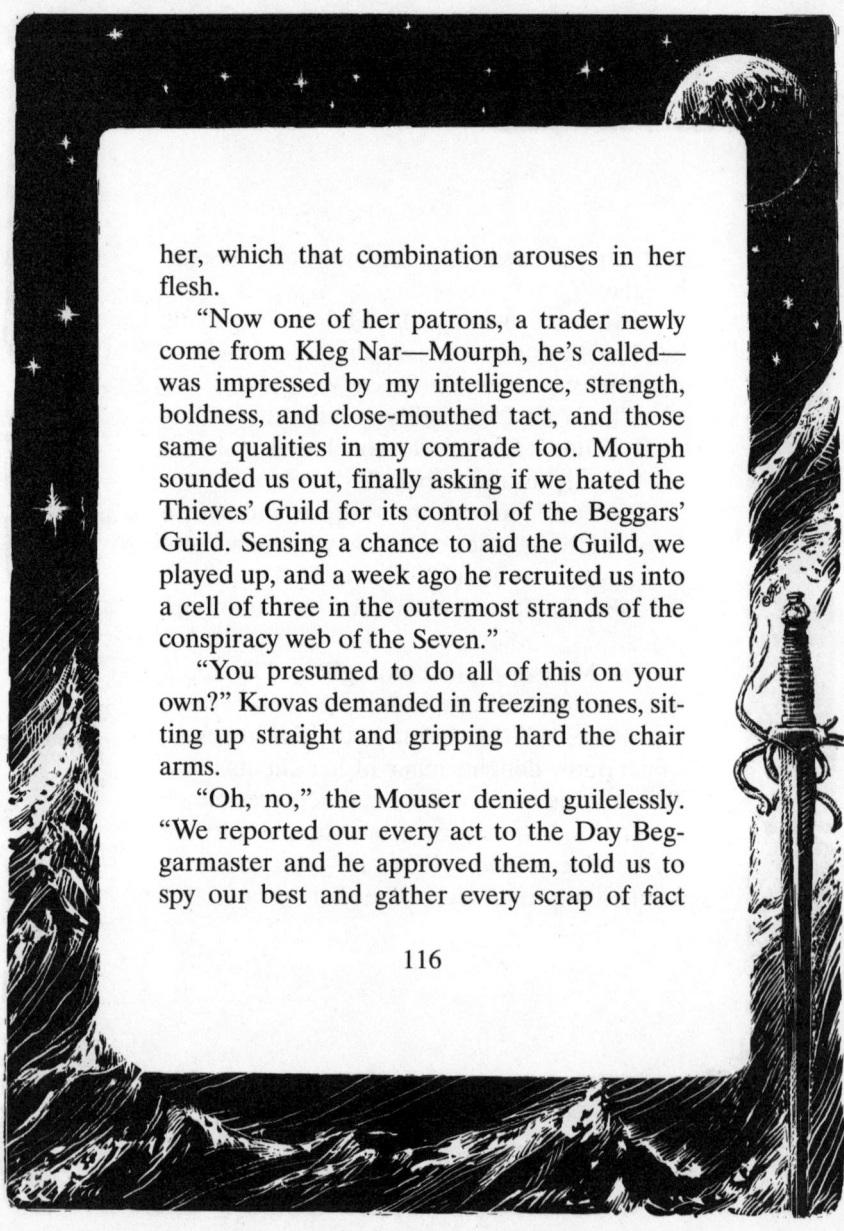

her, which that combination arouses in her flesh.

"Now one of her patrons, a trader newly come from Kleg Nar—Mourph, he's called—was impressed by my intelligence, strength, boldness, and close-mouthed tact, and those same qualities in my comrade too. Mourph sounded us out, finally asking if we hated the Thieves' Guild for its control of the Beggars' Guild. Sensing a chance to aid the Guild, we played up, and a week ago he recruited us into a cell of three in the outermost strands of the conspiracy web of the Seven."

"You presumed to do all of this on your own?" Krovas demanded in freezing tones, sitting up straight and gripping hard the chair arms.

"Oh, no," the Mouser denied guilelessly. "We reported our every act to the Day Beggarmaster and he approved them, told us to spy our best and gather every scrap of fact

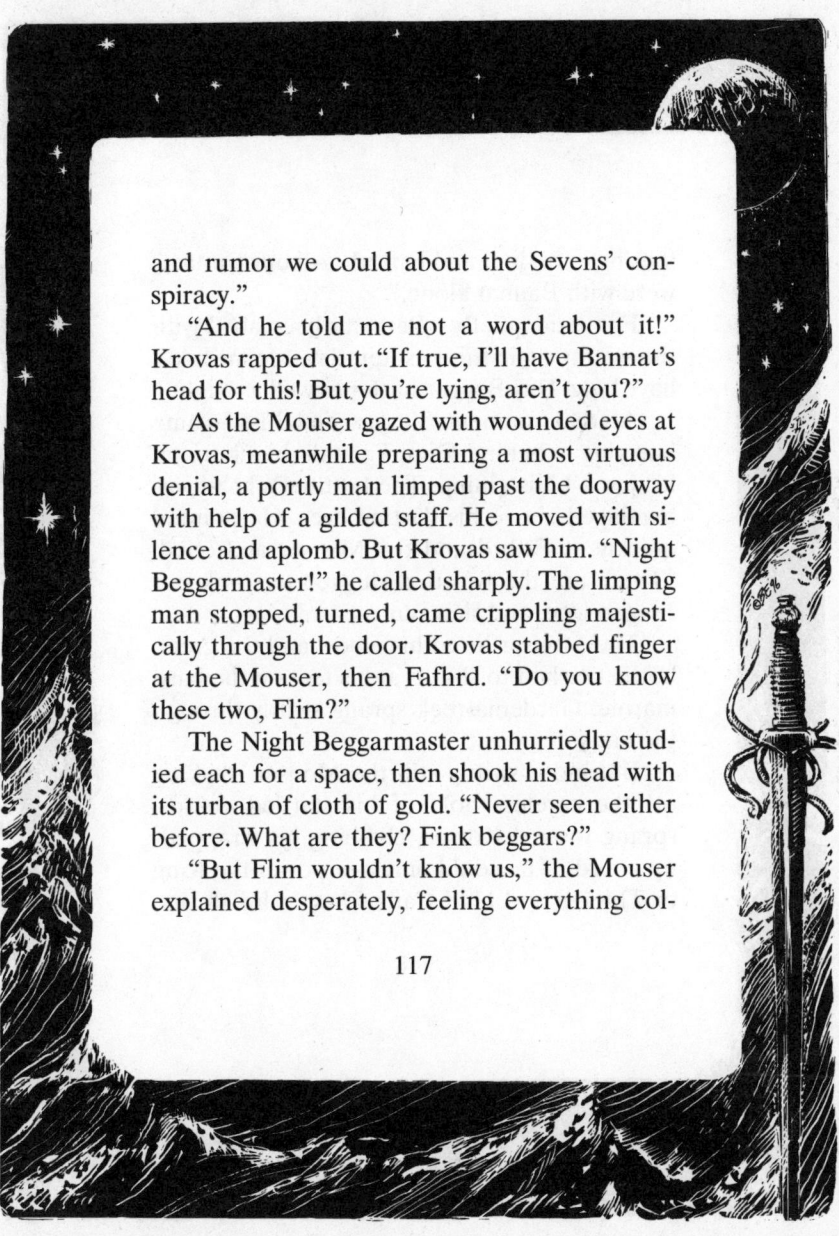

and rumor we could about the Sevens' conspiracy."

"And he told me not a word about it!" Krovas rapped out. "If true, I'll have Bannat's head for this! But you're lying, aren't you?"

As the Mouser gazed with wounded eyes at Krovas, meanwhile preparing a most virtuous denial, a portly man limped past the doorway with help of a gilded staff. He moved with silence and aplomb. But Krovas saw him. "Night Beggarmaster!" he called sharply. The limping man stopped, turned, came crippling majestically through the door. Krovas stabbed finger at the Mouser, then Fafhrd. "Do you know these two, Flim?"

The Night Beggarmaster unhurriedly studied each for a space, then shook his head with its turban of cloth of gold. "Never seen either before. What are they? Fink beggars?"

"But Flim wouldn't know us," the Mouser explained desperately, feeling everything collapsing in on him and Fafhrd. "All our contacts were with Bannat alone."

Flim said quietly, "Bannat's been abed with the swamp ague this past ten-day. Meanwhile *I* have been Day Beggarmaster as well as Night."

At that moment Slevyas and Fissif came hurrying in behind Flim. The tall thief bore on his jaw a bluish lump. The fat thief's head was bandaged above his darting eyes. He pointed quickly at Fafhrd and the Mouser and cried, "There are the two that slugged us, took our Jengao loot, and slew our escort."

The Mouser lifted his elbow and the green bottle crashed to shards at his feet on the hard marble. Gardenia-reek sprang swiftly through the air.

But more swiftly still the Mouser, shaking off the careless hold of his startled guards, sprang toward Krovas, clubbing his wrapped-up sword. If he could only overpower the King of Thieves and hold Cat's Claw at his throat, he'd be able to bargain for his and Fafhrd's lives. That is unless the other thieves wanted their master killed, which wouldn't surprise him at all.

With startling speed Flim thrust out his gilded staff, tripping the Mouser, who went heels over head, midway seeking to change his involuntary somersault into a voluntary one.

Meanwhile Fafhrd lurched heavily against his left-hand captor, at the same time swinging bandaged Graywand strongly upward to strike his right-hand captor under the jaw. Regaining his one-legged balance with a mighty contortion, he hopped for the loot-wall behind him.

Slevyas made for the wall of thieves' tools, and with a muscle-cracking effort wrenched the great pry-bar from its padlocked ring.

Scrambling to his feet after a poor landing in front of Krovas' chair, the Mouser found it empty and the Thief King in a half-crouch be-

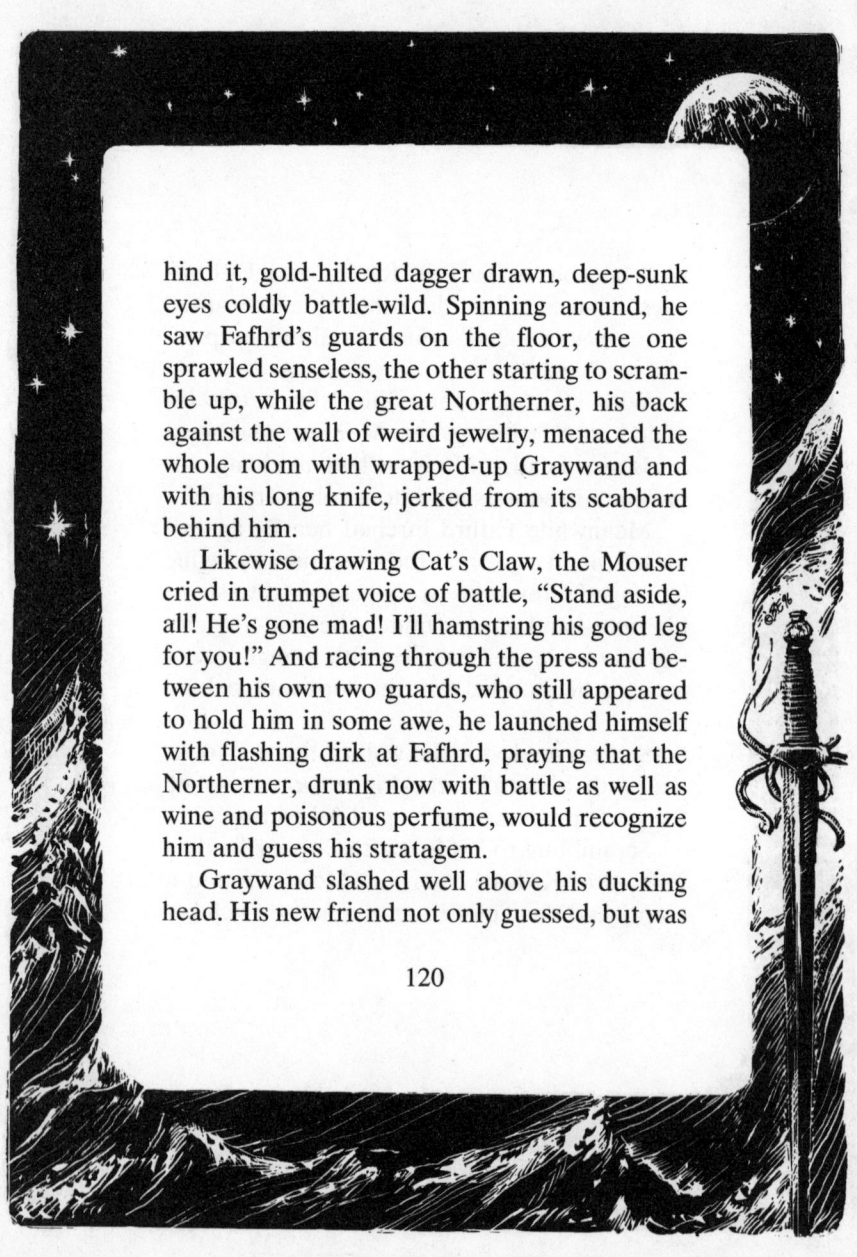

hind it, gold-hilted dagger drawn, deep-sunk eyes coldly battle-wild. Spinning around, he saw Fafhrd's guards on the floor, the one sprawled senseless, the other starting to scramble up, while the great Northerner, his back against the wall of weird jewelry, menaced the whole room with wrapped-up Graywand and with his long knife, jerked from its scabbard behind him.

Likewise drawing Cat's Claw, the Mouser cried in trumpet voice of battle, "Stand aside, all! He's gone mad! I'll hamstring his good leg for you!" And racing through the press and between his own two guards, who still appeared to hold him in some awe, he launched himself with flashing dirk at Fafhrd, praying that the Northerner, drunk now with battle as well as wine and poisonous perfume, would recognize him and guess his stratagem.

Graywand slashed well above his ducking head. His new friend not only guessed, but was playing up—and not just missing by accident, the Mouser hoped. Stooping low by the wall, he cut the lashings on Fafhrd's left leg. Graywand and Fafhrd's long knife continued to spare him. Springing up, he headed for the corridor, crying overshoulder to Fafhrd, "Come on!"

Hristomilo stood well out of his way, quietly observing. Fissif scuttled toward safety. Krovas stayed behind his chair, shouting, "Stop them! Head them off!"

The three remaining ruffian guards, at last beginning to recover their fighting-wits, gathered to oppose the Mouser. But menacing them with swift feints of his dirk, he slowed them and darted between—and then just in the nick of time knocked aside with a downsweep of wrapped-up Scalpel Flim's gilded staff, thrust once again to trip him.

All this gave Slevyas time to return from the tools-wall and aim at the Mouser a great

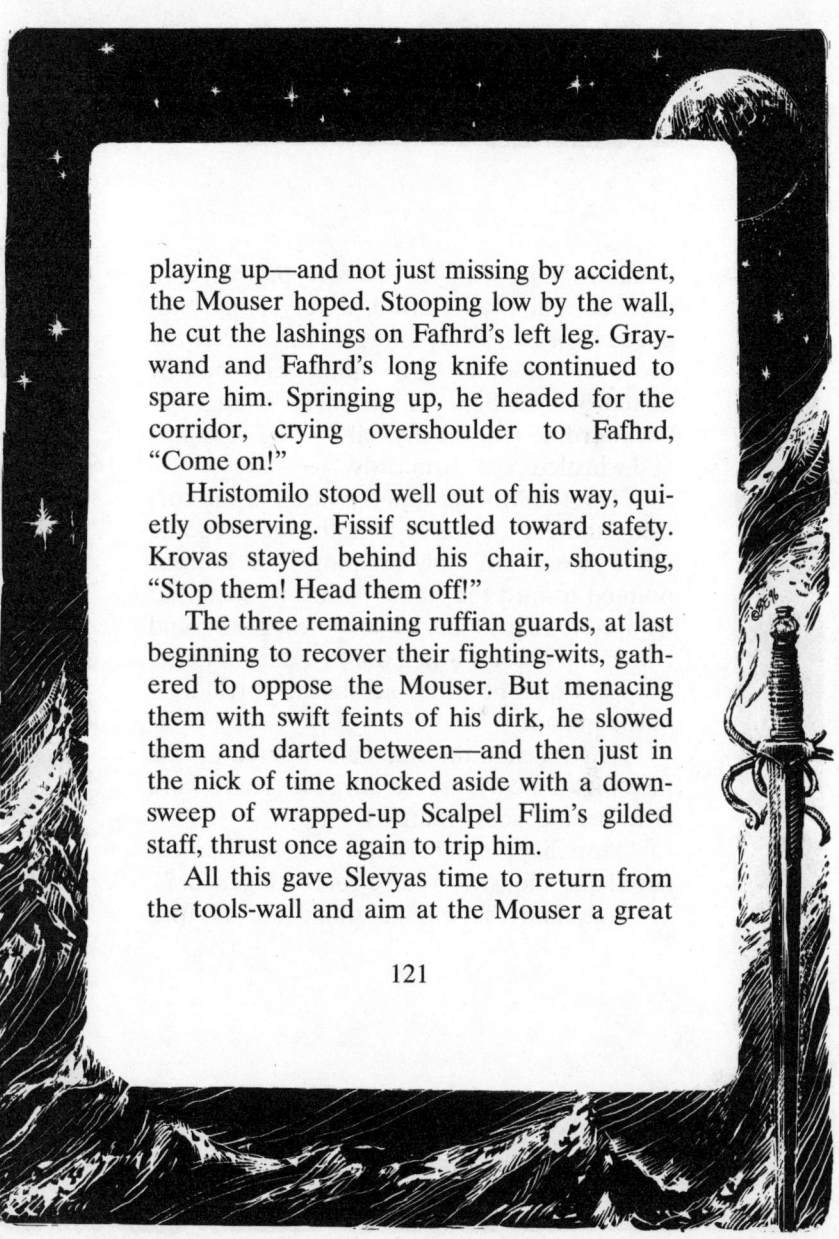

swinging blow with the massive pry-bar. But even as that blow started, a very long, bandaged sword on a very long arm thrust over the Mouser's shoulder and solidly and heavily poked Slevyas high on the chest, jolting him backward, so that the pry-bar's swing was short and whistled past harmlessly.

Then the Mouser found himself in the corridor and Fafhrd beside him, though for some weird reason still only hopping. The Mouser pointed toward the stairs. Fafhrd nodded, but delayed to reach high, still on one leg only, and rip off the nearest wall a dozen cubits of heavy drapes, which he threw across the corridor to baffle pursuit.

They reached the stairs and started up the next flight, the Mouser in advance. There were cries behind, some muffled.

"Stop hopping, Fafhrd!" the Mouser ordered querulously. "You've got two legs again."

"Yes, and the other's still dead," Fafhrd

complained. "Ahh! Now feeling begins to return to it."

A thrown knife whisked between them and dully clinked as it hit the wall point-first and stone-powder flew. Then they were around the bend.

Two more empty corridors, two more curving flights, and then they saw above them on the last landing a stout ladder mounting to a dark, square hole in the roof. A thief with hair bound back by a colorful handkerchief—it appeared to be a door guards' identification—menaced the Mouser with drawn sword, but when he saw that there were two of them, both charging him determinedly with shining knives and strange staves or clubs, he turned and ran down the last empty corridor.

The Mouser, followed closely by Fafhrd, rapidly mounted the ladder and without pause vaulted up through the hatch into the star-crusted night.

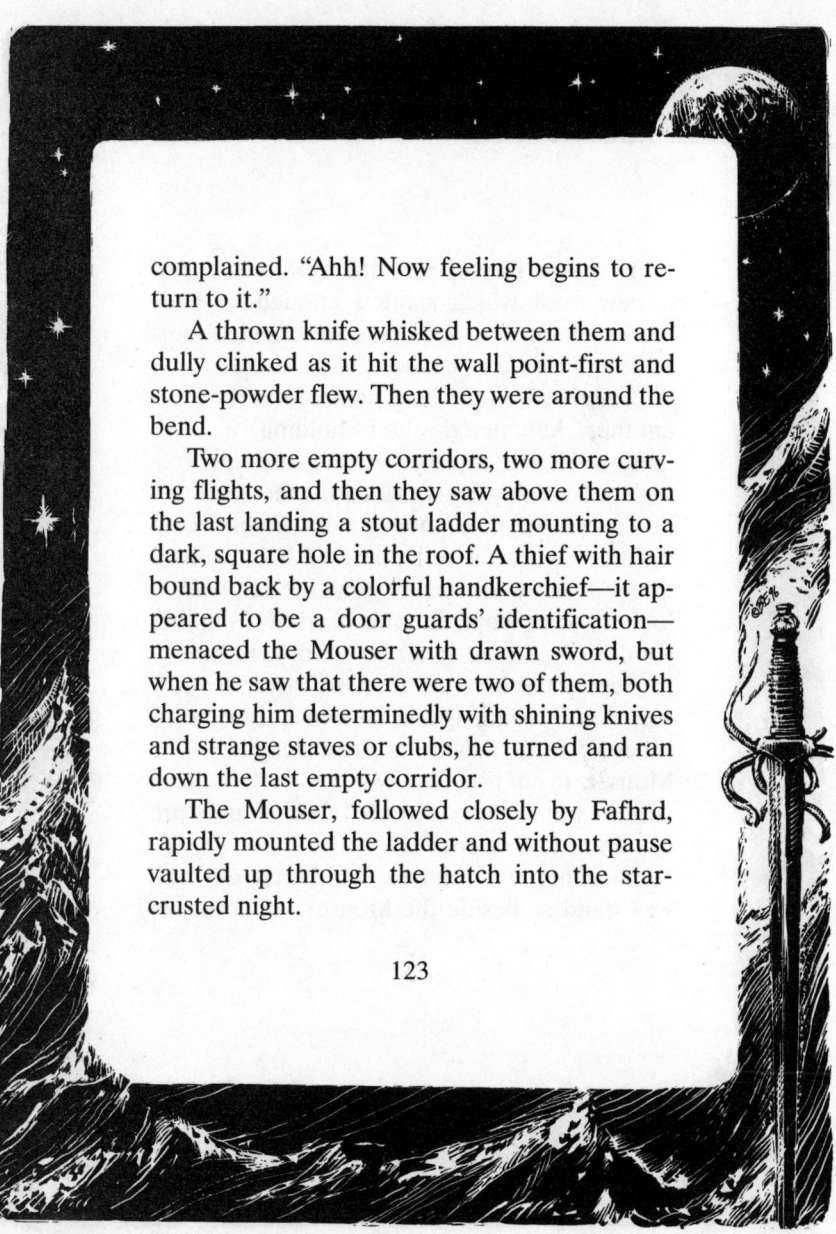

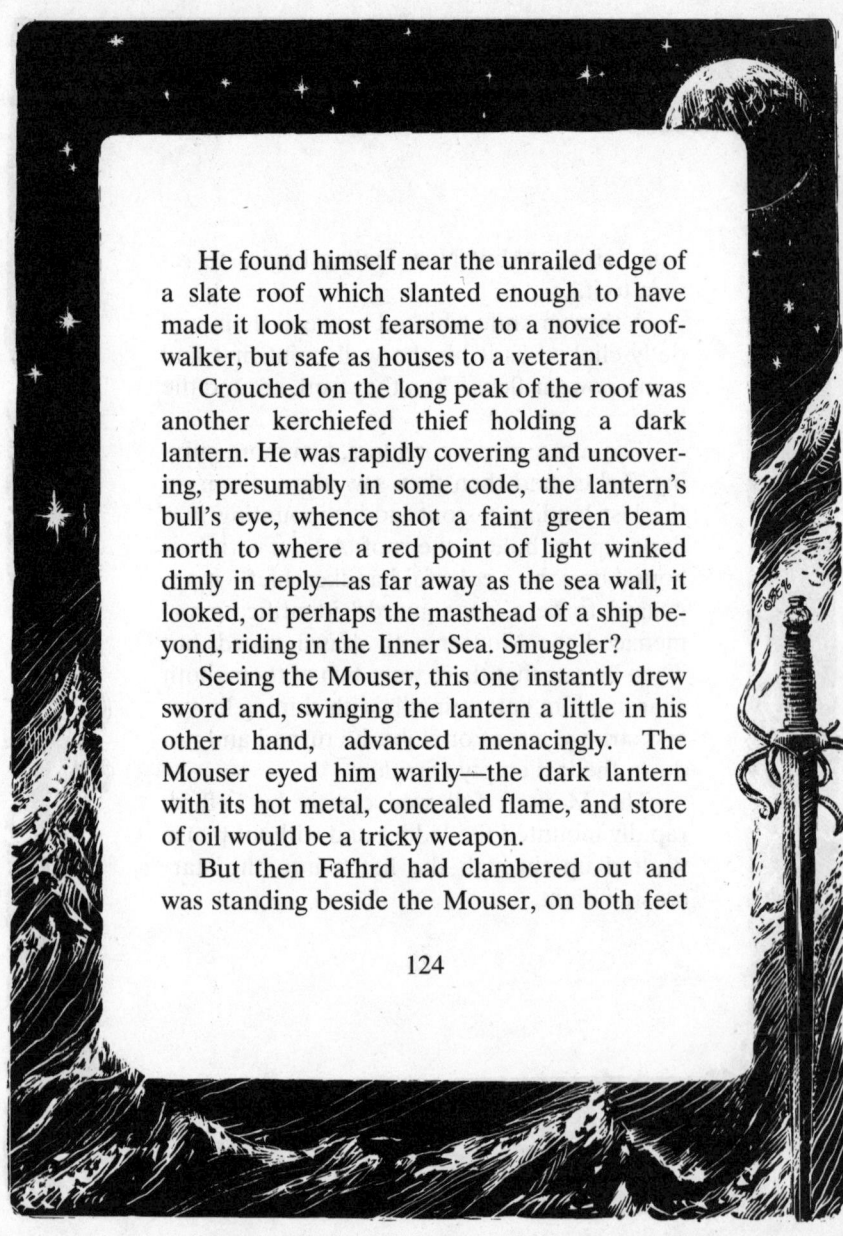

He found himself near the unrailed edge of a slate roof which slanted enough to have made it look most fearsome to a novice roof-walker, but safe as houses to a veteran.

Crouched on the long peak of the roof was another kerchiefed thief holding a dark lantern. He was rapidly covering and uncovering, presumably in some code, the lantern's bull's eye, whence shot a faint green beam north to where a red point of light winked dimly in reply—as far away as the sea wall, it looked, or perhaps the masthead of a ship beyond, riding in the Inner Sea. Smuggler?

Seeing the Mouser, this one instantly drew sword and, swinging the lantern a little in his other hand, advanced menacingly. The Mouser eyed him warily—the dark lantern with its hot metal, concealed flame, and store of oil would be a tricky weapon.

But then Fafhrd had clambered out and was standing beside the Mouser, on both feet again at last. Their adversary backed slowly away toward the north end of the roof ridge. Fleetingly the Mouser wondered if there was another hatch there.

Turning back at a bumping sound, he saw Fafhrd prudently hoisting the ladder. Just as he got it free, a knife flashed up close past him out of the hatch. While following its flight, the Mouser frowned, involuntarily admiring the skill required to hurl a knife vertically with any accuracy.

It clattered down near them and slid off the roof. The Mouser loped south across the slates and was halfway from the hatch to that end of the roof when the faint chink came of the knife striking the cobbles of Murder Alley.

Fafhrd followed more slowly, in part perhaps from a lesser experience of roofs, in part because he still limped a bit to favor his left leg, and in part because he was carrying the heavy ladder balanced on his right shoulder.

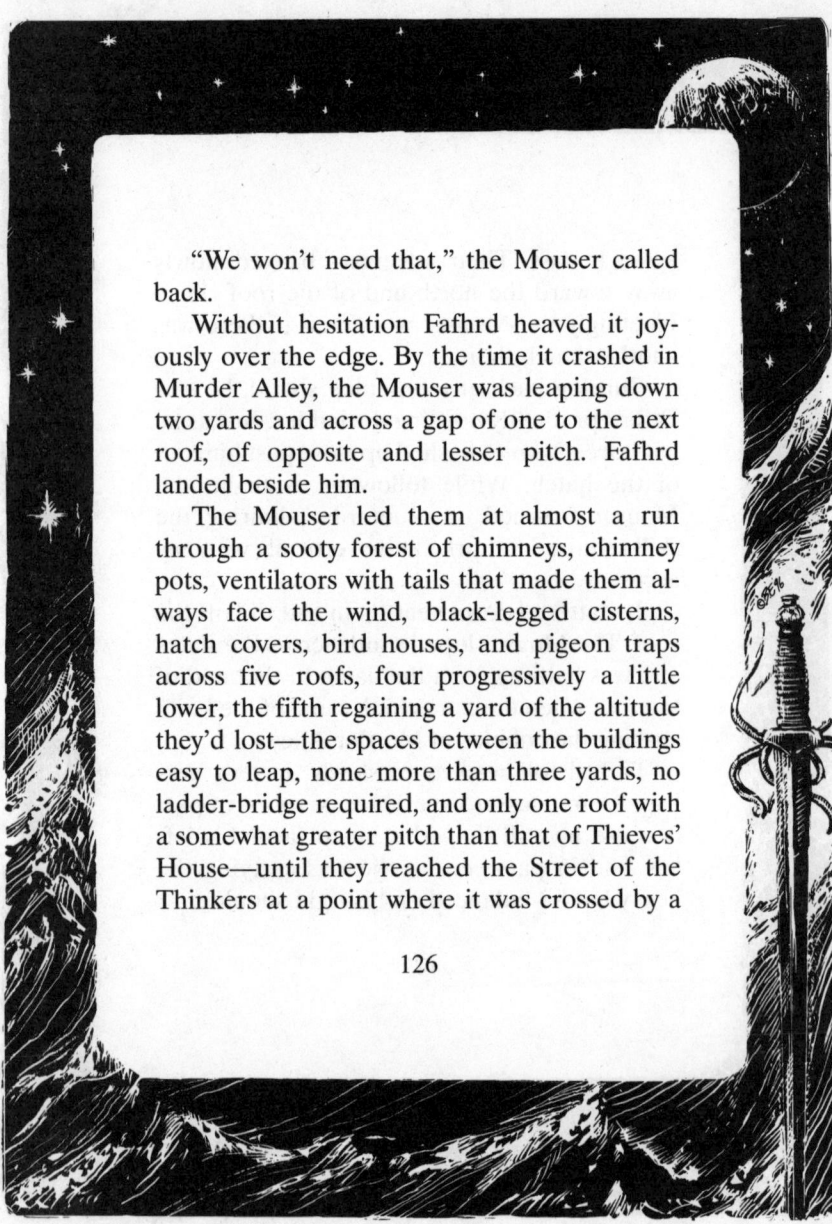

"We won't need that," the Mouser called back.

Without hesitation Fafhrd heaved it joyously over the edge. By the time it crashed in Murder Alley, the Mouser was leaping down two yards and across a gap of one to the next roof, of opposite and lesser pitch. Fafhrd landed beside him.

The Mouser led them at almost a run through a sooty forest of chimneys, chimney pots, ventilators with tails that made them always face the wind, black-legged cisterns, hatch covers, bird houses, and pigeon traps across five roofs, four progressively a little lower, the fifth regaining a yard of the altitude they'd lost—the spaces between the buildings easy to leap, none more than three yards, no ladder-bridge required, and only one roof with a somewhat greater pitch than that of Thieves' House—until they reached the Street of the Thinkers at a point where it was crossed by a

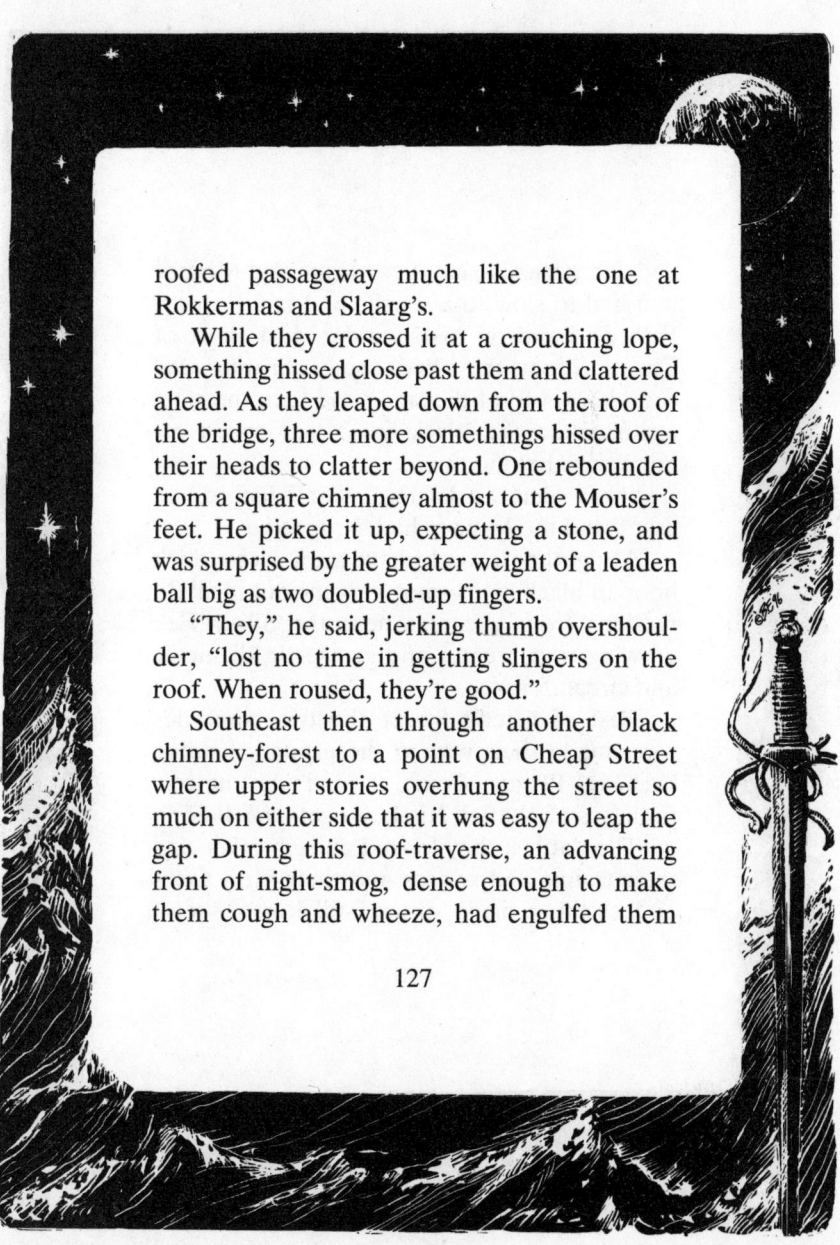

roofed passageway much like the one at Rokkermas and Slaarg's.

While they crossed it at a crouching lope, something hissed close past them and clattered ahead. As they leaped down from the roof of the bridge, three more somethings hissed over their heads to clatter beyond. One rebounded from a square chimney almost to the Mouser's feet. He picked it up, expecting a stone, and was surprised by the greater weight of a leaden ball big as two doubled-up fingers.

"They," he said, jerking thumb overshoulder, "lost no time in getting slingers on the roof. When roused, they're good."

Southeast then through another black chimney-forest to a point on Cheap Street where upper stories overhung the street so much on either side that it was easy to leap the gap. During this roof-traverse, an advancing front of night-smog, dense enough to make them cough and wheeze, had engulfed them

and for perhaps sixty heartbeats the Mouser had had to slow to a shuffle and feel his way, Fafhrd's hand on his shoulder. Just short of Cheap Street they had come abruptly and completely out of the smog and seen the stars again, while the black front had rolled off northward behind them.

"Now what the devil was that?" Fafhrd had asked and the Mouser had shrugged.

A nighthawk would have seen a vast thick hoop of black night-smog blowing out in all directions from a center near the Silver Eel, growing ever greater and greater in diameter and circumference.

East of Cheap Street the two comrades soon made their way to the ground, landing back in Plague Court behind the narrow premises of Nattick Nimblefingers the Tailor.

Then at last they looked at each other and their trammeled swords and their filthy faces and clothing made dirtier still by roof-soot, and they laughed and laughed and laughed. Fafhrd roaring still as he bent over to massage his left leg above and below knee. This hooting and wholly unaffected self-mockery continued while they unwrapped their swords—the Mouser as if his were a surprise package—and clipped their scabbards once more to their belts. Their exertions had burned out of them the last mote and atomy of strong wine and even stronger stenchful perfume, but they felt no desire whatever for more drink, only the urge to get home and eat hugely and guzzle hot, bitter gahveh, and tell their lovely girls at length the tale of their mad adventure.

They loped on side by side, at intervals glancing at each other and chuckling, though keeping a normally wary eye behind and before for pursuit or interception, despite their expecting neither.

Free of night-smog and drizzled with starlight, their cramped surroundings seemed

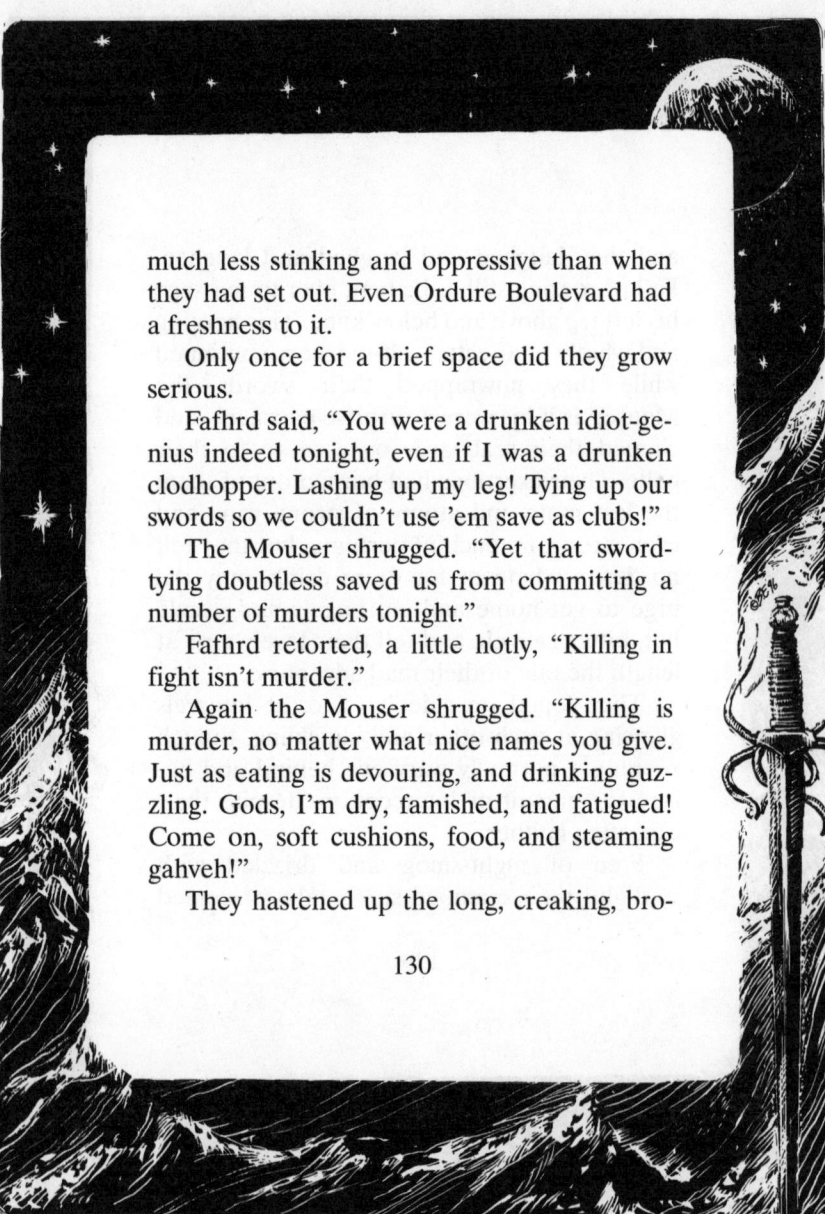

much less stinking and oppressive than when they had set out. Even Ordure Boulevard had a freshness to it.

Only once for a brief space did they grow serious.

Fafhrd said, "You were a drunken idiot-genius indeed tonight, even if I was a drunken clodhopper. Lashing up my leg! Tying up our swords so we couldn't use 'em save as clubs!"

The Mouser shrugged. "Yet that sword-tying doubtless saved us from committing a number of murders tonight."

Fafhrd retorted, a little hotly, "Killing in fight isn't murder."

Again the Mouser shrugged. "Killing is murder, no matter what nice names you give. Just as eating is devouring, and drinking guzzling. Gods, I'm dry, famished, and fatigued! Come on, soft cushions, food, and steaming gahveh!"

They hastened up the long, creaking, broken-treaded stairs with an easy carefulness and when they were both on the porch, the Mouser shoved at the door to open it with surprise-swiftness.

It did not budge.

"Bolted," he said to Fafhrd shortly. He noted now there was hardly any light at all coming through the cracks around the door, or noticeable through the lattices—at most, a faint orange-red glow. Then with sentimental grin and in a fond voice in which only the ghost of uneasiness lurked, he said, "They've gone to sleep, the unworrying wenches!" He knocked loudly thrice and then cupping his lips shouted softly at the door crack, "Hola, Ivrian! I'm home safe. Hail, Vlana! Your man's done you proud, felling Guild-thieves innumerable with one foot tied behind his back!"

There was no sound whatever from inside—that is, if one discounted a rustling so

faint it was impossible to be sure of it. Fafhrd was wrinkling his nostrils. "I smell smoke."

The Mouser banged on the door again. Still no response.

Fafhrd motioned him out of the way, hunching his big shoulder to crash the portal.

The Mouser shook his head and with a deft tap, slide, and tug removed a brick that a moment before had looked a firm-set part of the wall beside the door. He reached in all his arm. There was the scrape of a bolt being withdrawn, then another, then a third. He swiftly recovered his arm and the door swung fully inward at a touch.

But neither he nor Fafhrd rushed in at once, as both had intended to, for the indefinable scent of danger and the unknown came puffing out along with an increased reek of smoke and a slight sickening sweet scent that though female was no decent female perfume, and a musty-sour animal odor.

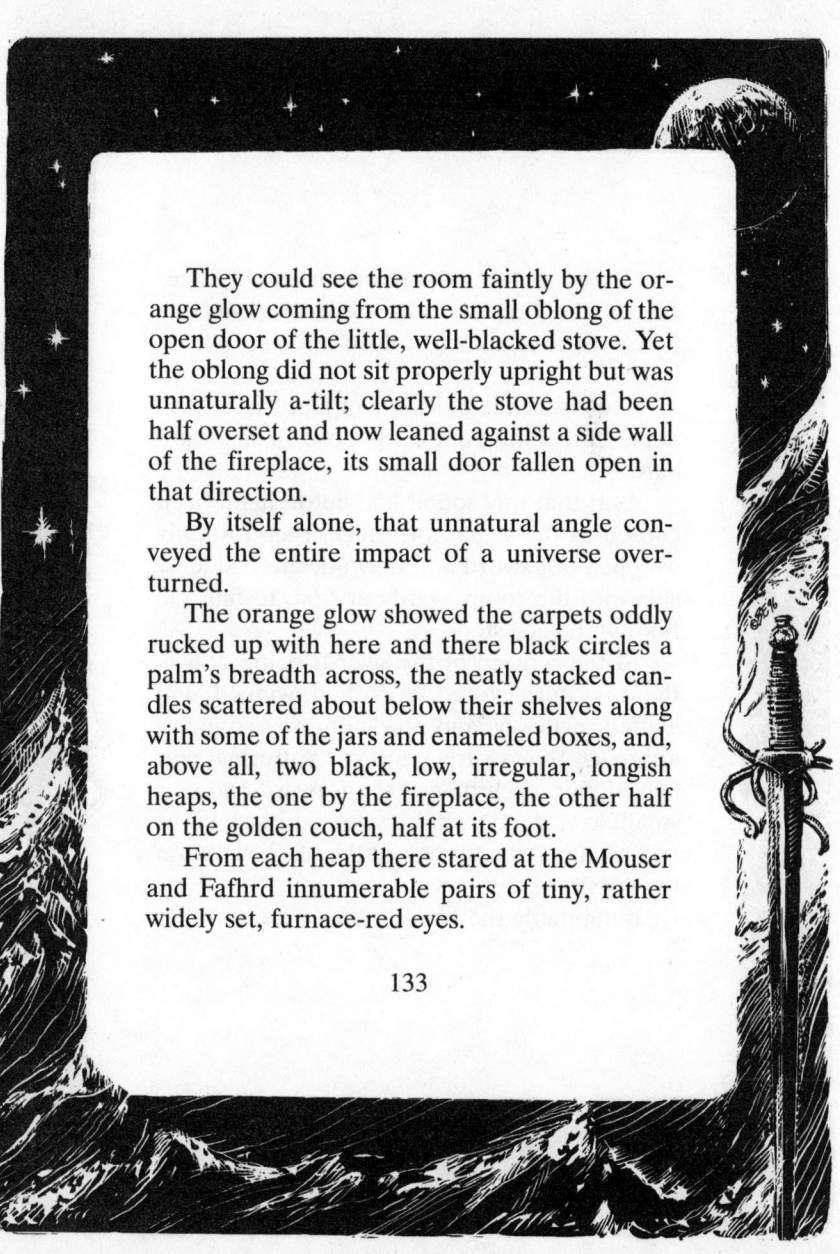

They could see the room faintly by the orange glow coming from the small oblong of the open door of the little, well-blacked stove. Yet the oblong did not sit properly upright but was unnaturally a-tilt; clearly the stove had been half overset and now leaned against a side wall of the fireplace, its small door fallen open in that direction.

By itself alone, that unnatural angle conveyed the entire impact of a universe overturned.

The orange glow showed the carpets oddly rucked up with here and there black circles a palm's breadth across, the neatly stacked candles scattered about below their shelves along with some of the jars and enameled boxes, and, above all, two black, low, irregular, longish heaps, the one by the fireplace, the other half on the golden couch, half at its foot.

From each heap there stared at the Mouser and Fafhrd innumerable pairs of tiny, rather widely set, furnace-red eyes.

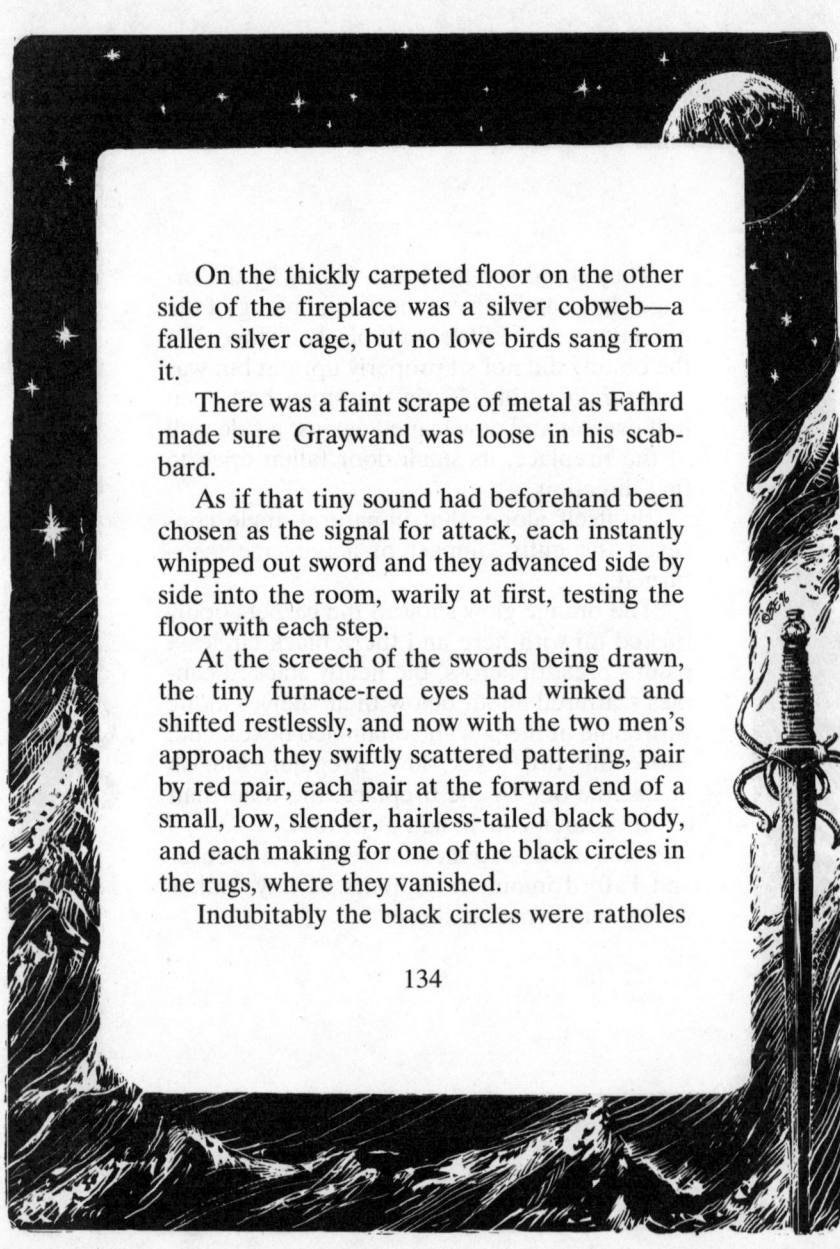

On the thickly carpeted floor on the other side of the fireplace was a silver cobweb—a fallen silver cage, but no love birds sang from it.

There was a faint scrape of metal as Fafhrd made sure Graywand was loose in his scabbard.

As if that tiny sound had beforehand been chosen as the signal for attack, each instantly whipped out sword and they advanced side by side into the room, warily at first, testing the floor with each step.

At the screech of the swords being drawn, the tiny furnace-red eyes had winked and shifted restlessly, and now with the two men's approach they swiftly scattered pattering, pair by red pair, each pair at the forward end of a small, low, slender, hairless-tailed black body, and each making for one of the black circles in the rugs, where they vanished.

Indubitably the black circles were ratholes

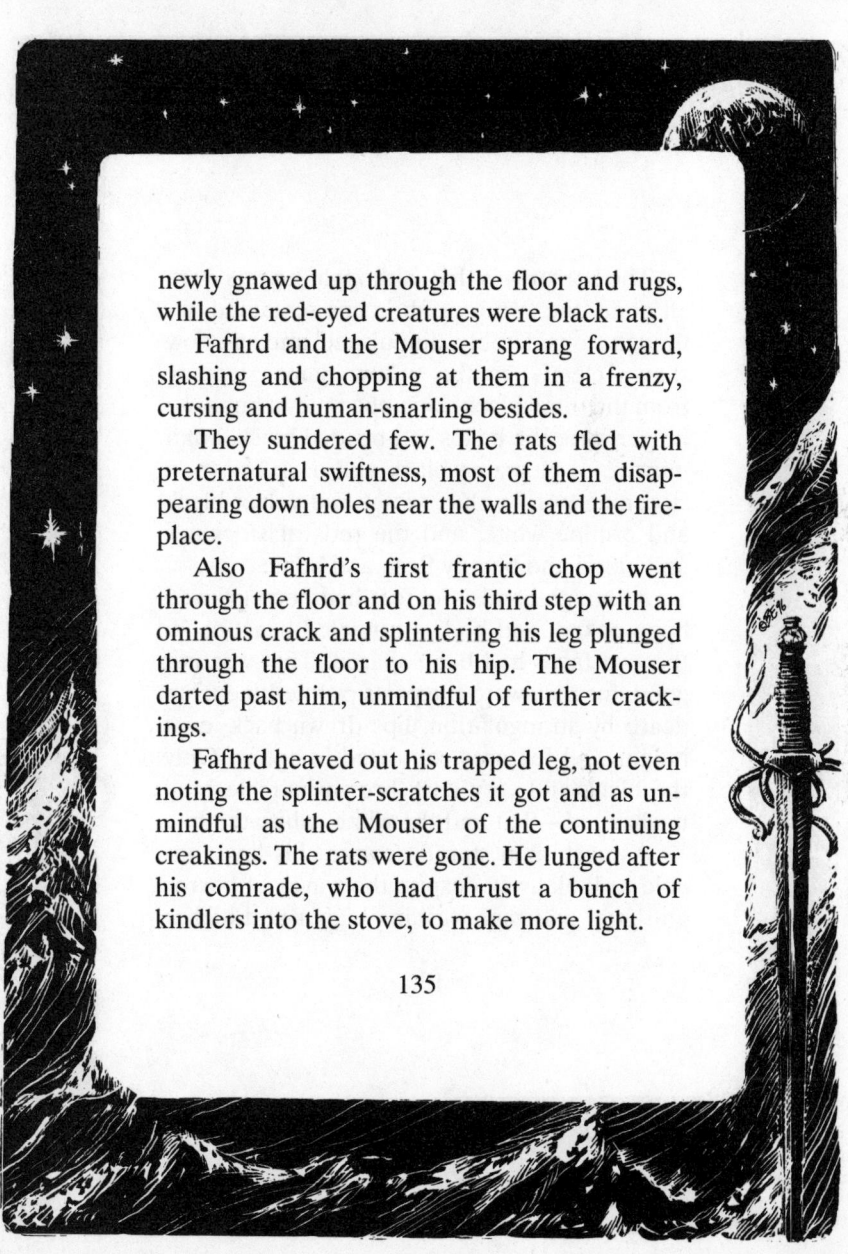

newly gnawed up through the floor and rugs, while the red-eyed creatures were black rats.

Fafhrd and the Mouser sprang forward, slashing and chopping at them in a frenzy, cursing and human-snarling besides.

They sundered few. The rats fled with preternatural swiftness, most of them disappearing down holes near the walls and the fireplace.

Also Fafhrd's first frantic chop went through the floor and on his third step with an ominous crack and splintering his leg plunged through the floor to his hip. The Mouser darted past him, unmindful of further crackings.

Fafhrd heaved out his trapped leg, not even noting the splinter-scratches it got and as unmindful as the Mouser of the continuing creakings. The rats were gone. He lunged after his comrade, who had thrust a bunch of kindlers into the stove, to make more light.

The horror was that, although the rats were all gone, the two longish heaps remained, although considerably diminished and, as now shown clearly by the yellow flames leaping from the tilted black door, changed in hue—no longer were the heaps red-beaded black, but a mixture of gleaming black and dark brown, a sickening purple-blue, violet and velvet black and ermine white, and the reds of stockings and blood and bloody flesh and bone.

Although hands and feet had been gnawed bone naked, and bodies tunneled heart-deep, the two faces had been spared. That was not good, for they were the parts purple-blue from death by strangulation, lips drawn back, eyes bulging, all features contorted in agony. Only the black and very dark brown hair gleamed unchanged—that and the white, white teeth.

As each man stared down at his love, unable to look away despite the waves of horror and grief and rage washing higher and higher in him, each saw a tiny black strand uncurl from the black depression ringing each throat and drift off, dissipating, toward the open door behind them—two strands of night-smog.

With a crescendo of crackings the floor sagged fully three spans more in the center before arriving at a new temporary stability.

Edges of centrally tortured minds noted details: that Vlana's silver-hilted dagger skewered to the floor a rat, which, likely enough, overeager had approached too closely before the night-smog had done its magic work. That her belt and pouch were gone. That the blue-enameled box inlaid with silver, in which Ivrian had put the Mouser's share of the highjacked jewels, was gone too.

The Mouser and Fafhrd lifted to each other white, drawn faces which were quite mad, yet completely joined in understanding and purpose. No need to tell each other what must have happened here when the two nooses of black vapor had jerked tight in Hristomilo's receiver, or why Slivikin had bounced and squeaked in glee, or the significance of such phrases as "an ample sufficiency of feasters," or "forget not the loot," or "that business we spoke of." No need for Fafhrd to explain why he now stripped off his robe and hood, or why he jerked up Vlana's dagger, snapped the rat off it with a wrist-flick, and thrust it in his belt. No need for the Mouser to tell why he searched out a half dozen jars of oil and after smashing three of them in front of the flaming stove, paused, thought, and stuck the other three in the sack at his waist, adding to them the remaining kindlers and the fire-pot, brimmed with red coals, its top lashed down tight.

Then, still without word exchanged, the Mouser muffled his hand with a small rug and reaching into the fireplace deliberately tipped the flaming stove forward, so that it fell door-down on oil-soaked rugs. Yellow flames sprang up around him.

They turned and raced for the door. With louder crackings than any before, the floor collapsed. They desperately scrambled their way up a steep hill of sliding carpets and reached door and porch just before all behind them gave way and the flaming rugs and stove and all the firewood and candles and the golden couch and all the little tables and boxes and jars—and the unthinkably mutilated bodies of their first loves—cascaded into the dry, dusty, cobweb-choked room below, and the great flames of a cleansing or at least obliterating cremation began to flare upward.

They plunged down the stairs, which tore away from the wall and collapsed and dully crashed in the dark just as they reached the ground. They had to fight their way over the wreckage to get to Bones Alley.

By then flames were darting their bright

lizard-tongues out of the shuttered attic windows and the boarded-up ones in the story just below. By the time they reached Plague Court, running side by side at top speed, the Silver Eel's fire-alarm was clanging cacophonously behind them.

They were still sprinting when they took the Death Alley fork. Then the Mouser grappled Fafhrd and forced him to a halt. The big man struck out, cursing insanely, and only desisted—his white face still a lunatic's—when the Mouser cried, panting, "Only ten heartbeats to arm us!"

He pulled the sack from his belt and, keeping tight hold of its neck, crashed it on the cobbles—hard enough to smash not only the bottles of oil, but also the fire-pot, for the sack was soon flaming a little at its base.

Then he drew gleaming Scalpel and Fafhrd Graywand and they raced on, the Mouser swinging his sack in a great circle beside him to

fan its flames. It was a veritable ball of fire burning his left hand as they dashed across Cheap Street and into Thieves' House, and the Mouser, leaping high, swung it up into the great niche above the doorway and let go of it.

The niche-guards screeched in surprise and pain at the fiery invader of their hidey hole and had no time to do anything with their swords, or whatever weapons else they had, against the other two invaders.

Student thieves poured out of the doors ahead at the screeching and foot-pounding, and then poured back as they saw the fierce point of flames and the two demon-faced oncomers brandishing their long, shining swords.

One skinny little apprentice—he could hardly have been ten years old—lingered too long. Graywand thrust him pitilessly through as his big eyes bulged and his small mouth gaped in horror and plea to Fafhrd for mercy.

Now from ahead of them there came a

weird, wailing call, hollow and hair-raising, and doors began to thus shut instead of spewing forth the armed guards they almost prayed would appear to be skewered by their swords. Also, despite the long, bracketed torches looking newly renewed, the corridor was dark.

The reason for this last became clear as they plunged up the stairs. Strands of nightsmog were appearing in the well, materializing from nothing or the air.

The strands grew longer and more numerous and tangible. They touched and clung nastily. In the corridor above they were forming from wall to wall and from ceiling to floor, like a gigantic cobweb, and were becoming so substantial that the Mouser and Fafhrd had to slash them to get through, or so their two maniac minds believed. The black web muffled a little a repetition of the eerie, wailing call, which came from the seventh door ahead and this time ended in a gleeful chittering and cackling insane as the emotions of the two attackers.

Here too doors were thudding shut. In an ephemeral flash of rationality, it occurred to the Mouser that it was not he and Fafhrd the thieves feared, for they had not been seen yet, but rather Hristomilo and his magic, even though working in defense of Thieves' House.

Even the map room, whence counter-attack would most likely erupt, was closed off by a huge oaken, iron-studded door.

They were now twice slashing black, clinging, rope-thick spiderweb for every single step they drove themselves forward. Midway between the map and magic rooms, there was forming on the inky web, ghostly at first but swiftly growing more substantial, a black spider big as a wolf.

The Mouser slashed heavy cobweb before it, dropped back two steps, then hurled himself at it in a high leap. Scalpel thrust through it, striking amidst its eight new-formed jet eyes, and it collapsed like a daggered bladder, loosing a vile stink.

Then he and Fafhrd were looking into the magic room, the alchemist's chamber. It was much as they had seen it before, except some things were doubled, or multiplied even further.

On the long table two blue-boiled cucurbits bubbled and roiled, their heads shooting out a solid, writhing rope more swiftly than moves the black swamp-cobra, which can run down a man—and not into twin receivers, but into the open air of the room (if any of the air in Thieves' House could have been called open then) to weave a barrier between their swords and Hristomilo, who once more stood tall though hunchbacked over his sorcerous, brown parchment, though this time his exultant gaze was chiefly fixed on Fafhrd and the

Mouser, with only an occasional downward glance at the text of the spell he drummingly intoned.

At the other end of the table, in the web-free space, there bounced not only Slivikin, but also a huge rat matching him in size in all members except the head.

From the ratholes at the foot of the walls red eyes glittered and gleamed in pairs.

With a bellow of rage Fafhrd began slashing at the black barrier, but the ropes were replaced from the cucurbit heads as swiftly as he sliced them, while the cut ends, instead of drooping slackly, now began to strain hungrily toward him like constrictive snakes or strangle-vines.

He suddenly shifted Graywand to his left hand, drew his long knife and hurled it at the sorcerer. Flashing toward its mark, it cut through three strands, was deflected and slowed by a fourth and fifth, almost halted by a sixth, and ended hanging futilely in the curled grip of a seventh.

Hristomilo laughed cacklingly and grinned, showing his huge upper incisors, while Slivikin chittered in ecstasy and bounded the higher.

The Mouser hurled Cat's Claw with no better result—worse, indeed, since his action gave two darting smog-strands time to curl hamperingly around his sword-hand and stranglingly around his neck. Black rats came racing out of the big holes at the cluttered base of the walls.

Meanwhile other strands snaked around Fafhrd's ankles, knees and left arm, almost toppling him. But even as he fought for balance, he jerked Vlana's dagger from his belt and raised it over his shoulder, its silver hilt glowing, its blade brown with dried rat's-blood.

The grin left Hristomilo's face as he saw it. The sorcerer screamed strangely and importuningly then and drew back from his parch-

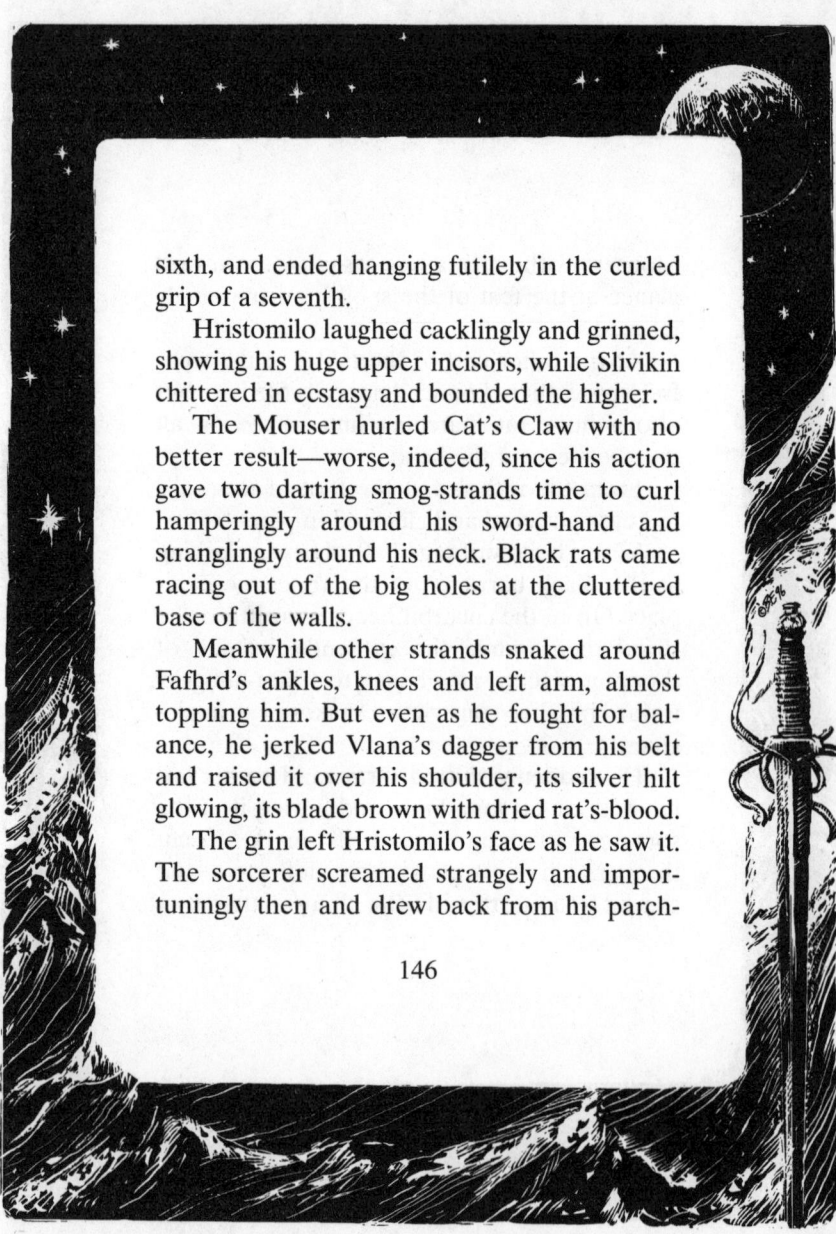

ment and the table, and raised clawed clubhands to ward off doom.

Vlana's dagger sped unimpeded through the black web—its strands even seemed to part for it—and betwixt the sorcerer's warding hands, to bury itself to the hilt in his right eye.

He screamed thinly in dire agony and clawed at his face.

The black web writhed as if in death spasm.

The cucurbits shattered as one, spilling their lava on the scarred table, putting out the blue flames even as the thick wood of the table began to smoke a little at the lava's edge. Lava dropped with *plops* on the dark marble floor.

With a faint, final scream Hristomilo pitched forward, hands still clutched to his eyes above his jutting nose, silver dagger-hilt still protruding between his fingers.

The web grew faint, like wet ink washed with a gush of clear water.

The Mouser raced forward and transfixed

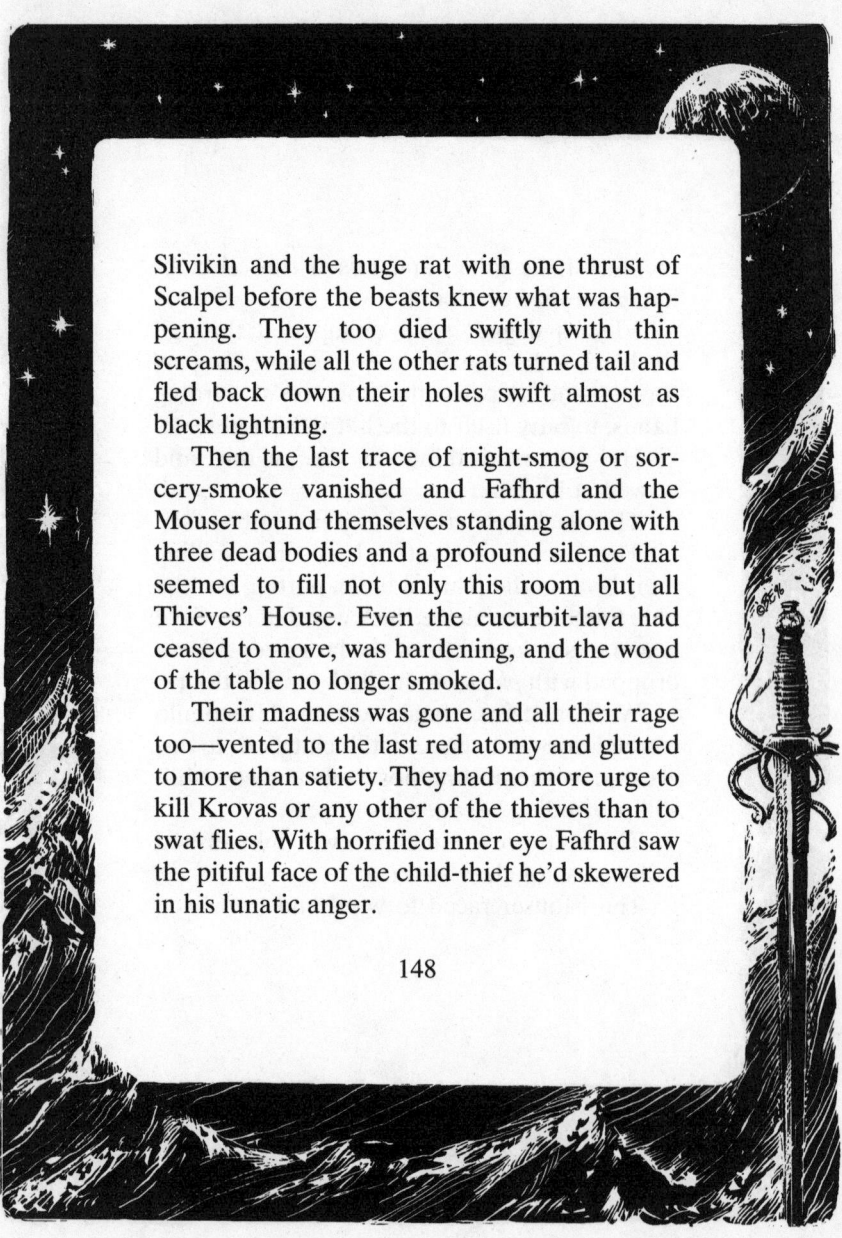

Slivikin and the huge rat with one thrust of Scalpel before the beasts knew what was happening. They too died swiftly with thin screams, while all the other rats turned tail and fled back down their holes swift almost as black lightning.

Then the last trace of night-smog or sorcery-smoke vanished and Fafhrd and the Mouser found themselves standing alone with three dead bodies and a profound silence that seemed to fill not only this room but all Thieves' House. Even the cucurbit-lava had ceased to move, was hardening, and the wood of the table no longer smoked.

Their madness was gone and all their rage too—vented to the last red atomy and glutted to more than satiety. They had no more urge to kill Krovas or any other of the thieves than to swat flies. With horrified inner eye Fafhrd saw the pitiful face of the child-thief he'd skewered in his lunatic anger.

Only their grief remained with them, diminished not one whit, but rather growing greater—that and an ever more swiftly growing revulsion from all that was around them: the dead, the disordered magic room, all Thieves' House, all of the city of Lankhmar to its last stinking alleyway and smog-wreathed spire.

With a hiss of disgust the Mouser jerked Scalpel from the rodent cadavers, wiped it on the nearest cloth, and returned it to its scabbard. Fafhrd likewise sketchily cleansed and sheathed Graywand. Then the two men picked up their knife and dirk from where they'd dropped to the floor when the web had dematerialized, though neither so much as glanced at Vlana's dagger where it was buried. But on the sorcerer's table they did notice Vlana's black velvet, silver-worked pouch and belt, the latter half overrun by the hardened black lava, and Ivrian's blue-enameled box inlaid with silver. From these they took the gems of Jengao.

With no more word than they had exchanged back at the Mouser's burned nest behind the Eel, but with a continuing sense of their unity of purpose, their identity of intent, and of their comradeship, they made their way with shoulders bowed and with slow, weary steps which only very gradually quickened out of the magic room and down the thick-carpeted corridor, past the map room's wide door still barred with oak and iron, and past all the other shut, silent doors—clearly the entire Guild was terrified of Hristomilo, his spells, and his rats; down the echoing stairs, their footsteps speeding a little; down the bare-floored lower corridor past its closed, quiet doors, their footsteps resounding loudly no matter how softly they sought to tread; under the deserted, black-scorched guard-niche, and so out into Cheap Street, turning left and

north because that was the nearest way to the Street of the Gods, and there turning right and east—not a waking soul in the wide street except for one skinny, bent-backed apprentice lad unhappily swabbing the flagstones in front of a wine shop in the dim pink light beginning to seep from the east, although there were many forms asleep, a-snore and a-dream in the gutters and under the dark porticos—yes, turning right and east down the Street of the Gods, for that way was the Marsh Gate, leading to Causey Road across the Great Salt Marsh, and the Marsh Gate was the nearest way out of the great and glamorous city that was now loathsome to them, indeed, not to be endured for one more stabbing, leaden heartbeat than was necessary—a city of beloved, unfaceable ghosts.

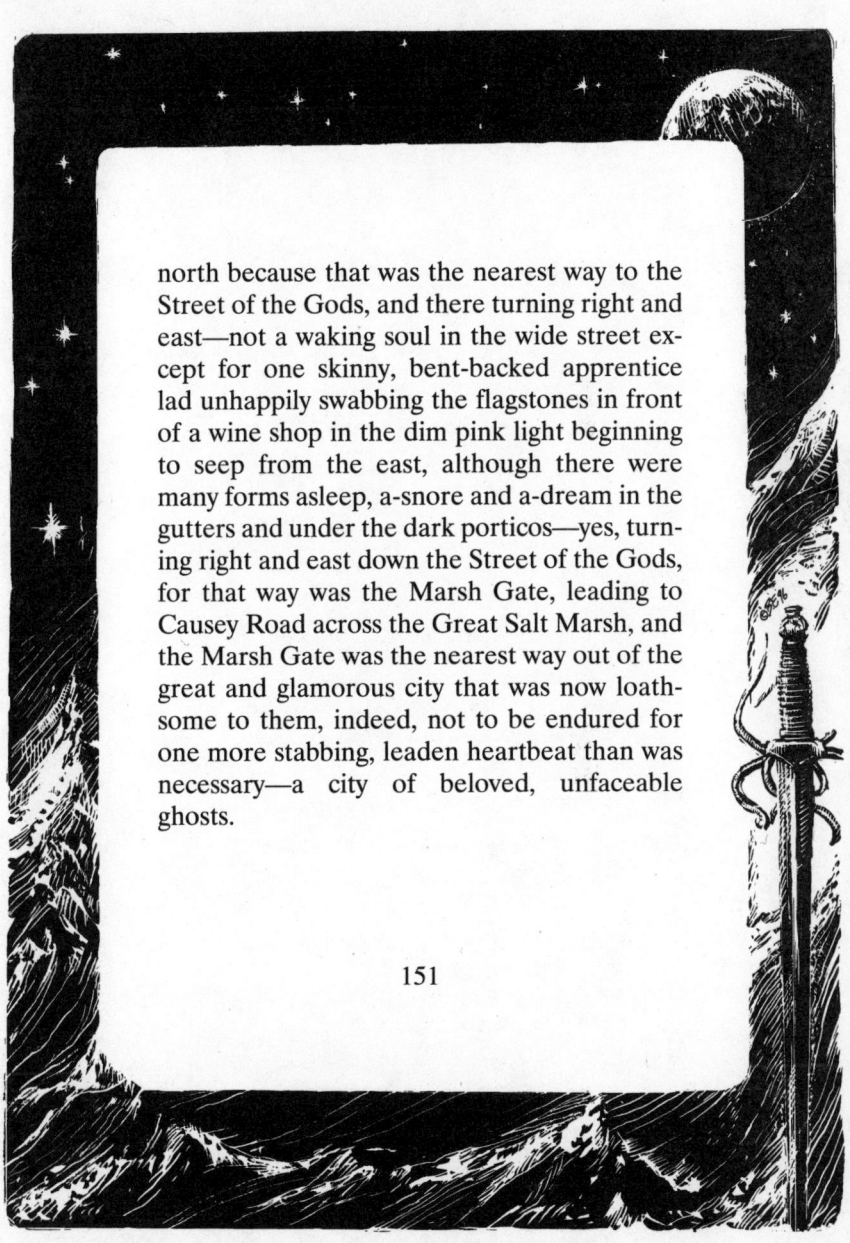